THE CEO

CYNTHIA WOOLF

Copyright © 2024 by Cynthia Woolf

All Rights Reserved. No part of this book may be reproduced or transmitted in any form or by any means, electrical, digital or mechanical including but not limited to photocopying, recording, scanning or by any type of data storage and retrieval system without express, written permission from the author.
This book was written by a human and not by AI.
No part of this book may be use to train AI.

Published by Firehouse Publishing
Woolf, Cynthia

Cover design copyright © 2024 Lori Jackson Design

STAY CONNECTED!

Newsletter
Want to hear about coming books first?
Sign up for my <u>newsletter</u> and get a free book.

Follow Cynthia

https://facebook.com/CynthiaWoolf
https://twitter.com/CynthiaWoolf
http://cynthiawoolf.com

Don't forget if you love the book, I'd appreciate it if you could leave a review at the retailer you purchased the book from.
Thanks so much,
Cynthia

PROLOGUE

*J*uly, three years ago, Denver, Colorado

KNOCK! Knock! Knock!

Bree Taylor looked at the clock on the microwave. Her coffee was almost done. Six o'clock in the morning. Who in the world would be at her door now? She gathered her chenille robe tighter about her and headed to the door. After looking through the peephole, she opened the door. "Yes. Can I help you?"

"Brianna Taylor?" asked the Marine captain in dress blues with his hat under his arm and wearing white gloves.

Behind him stood another marine and a chaplain, both in their regular uniforms.

"I am." She shook her head. This couldn't be

happening. Her eyes filled with tears. Only one thing would bring these three men to her doorstep…Brad.

"Miss Taylor—"

"No. No. No." She continued shaking her head. This wasn't real. "No!"

The officer continued, "I'm sorry to inform you that your fiancé Bradford Anderson was killed while on active duty in Afghanistan this past Monday. You are listed as his only next of kin."

Her heart hurt. Bree grabbed the door handle as it was the only thing to latch on to.

The captain stepped forward and took her by the arm. "Perhaps we should go inside."

She nodded. "Yes, that would be best." Bree straightened her back. She worried this day could come every time Brad deployed to some war-torn part of the planet, but she didn't think it would happen so soon. He'd only been gone for two months. She sat on the sofa and looked up at the officer. "What's your name?"

He stood with his hat under his arm. "Captain Marcus O'Reilly."

"You must hate this part of your job."

"Yes, ma'am. It is never easy informing loved ones at a time like this. Can I get you some water or something?"

His voice was muffled. Bree shook her head. "No. Nothing. How did it happen?" She was barely keeping the tears at bay, but she needed answers. "Please sit, so I'm not looking up at you."

He nodded. His hair was dark above the white sidewalls of the military cut. He sat and angled his body toward her. "It was an IED. That's how many of our soldiers die. They are insidious. If it's any consolation, he didn't suffer."

She nodded and held back another sob.

"Is there someone I can call for you? You really shouldn't be alone at a time like this."

Swallowing hard, she nodded. "Adam. Adam Kincaid. He's Brad's best friend."

"Do you have the number for Mr. Kincaid?"

"Yes, let me..." She picked up the phone on the coffee table, then unlocked the phone before handing it back to the captain. "He's on my favorites list, the second name."

The captain took her phone and touched the favorites list and then Adam's name. He put it on speaker.

She heard Adam curse at being woken up. It was Saturday, the only day of the week he allowed himself to sleep in. Despite the situation, she smiled at the normalcy of his response.

"Bree? What's wrong?"

The captain glanced at Bree. "Mr. Kincaid, this is Captain Marcus O'Reilly with the Marine Corps. I believe that you should come over to Miss Taylor's as soon as possible."

"What happened? It's Brad, isn't it? Never mind. I'll be there in fifteen minutes. Or less."

"Thank you, Adam," said Bree with a sob and her arms clasped over her stomach. Holding it together was getting harder and harder with each passing minute. She would never have the perfect ranch house on acreage with horses and chickens and two dogs for the kids to play with. Never have the four kids she and Brad had planned on. Never have the wedding she'd dreamed of with the perfect dress to go along with the perfect groom. And Brad would have been the perfect groom. He was the perfect everything…to her. How could she go on without him, without their dreams, without holding each other every night and again in the morning?

Nothing would be the same, and she had no future without Brad. How could she go on?

About ten minutes later, a knock sounded.

The captain stood and walked to the door.

Adam rushed past the captain to Bree.

She lost it and buried her face in his chest, her arms around his waist, as tears rolled down her face and she bawled.

Adam picked her up in his arms and sat her on his lap.

He buried his face in her hair.

She felt rather than heard his sobs. He and Brad had been best friends since kindergarten. He was hurting as much as she was. They had both lost their best friend.

"May I leave you here, sir, to care for Miss Taylor?" asked Captain O'Reilly.

Bree lifted her head and spoke to the captain. "Adam will stay. You don't have to worry about me. I'll be fine." Though she said the words, she knew they were a lie. She would never be fine again.

* * *

DRIVING THE LAMBORGHINI, Adam raced to Bree's, breaking every speed limit to get to her side. He'd left Valerie home, but it didn't matter. They were divorcing anyway, and Bree needed him. He knew she would be a mess. Heck, *he* was a mess. Brad. Gone. He couldn't wrap his mind around it.

After Adam finished his stint with the Navy SEALs, he'd tried to get Brad to join him when he started Kincaid Holdings. It would have been Kincaid and Anderson Holdings then. Brad would have been a richer man now, if he had. But he'd wanted to be a Marine since second grade, when one came to talk to the class. He'd decided then and there that he would wear that uniform and carry a sword. And he'd done it.

Joined right out of high school. He'd worked his way up to captain in the fourteen years he'd been in.

Adam was proud of him.

Brad was happy, and then he met Bree, and together they were his best friends and the happiest couple he'd ever seen.

That made him even bitterer about his own marriage, which was ending in divorce. He wondered now if he'd ever loved Valerie. He'd always put Bree's needs before hers. He realized now that he always would. Bree was his best friend, along with Brad. Now, his only best friend.

Pushing that out of his mind, he focused on Bree as he knocked on her door.

When the captain answered, Adam rushed to Bree on the sofa. She just looked at him and tears ran from her eyes down her sweet cheeks. He hated seeing her like this, but knew she needed to get the immediate grieving process started. As did he.

He held her and when he sat her on his lap; she buried her head in his chest.

Adam couldn't hold his tears any longer and leaned his forehead against the top of her head and let them flow.

The captain asked if Adam would stay and take care of Bree.

She'd answered for him and said he'd stay.

And he would, for as long as she needed him. He would cancel everything else to be with Bree and help her get past this.

He needed her as much as she needed him at this moment in time. He would keep his promise to Brad to take care of Bree if anything happened to him. Brad was no one's fool. He had his business in order before he took off. That meant his will and his financial records and accounts were all in order and ready for Adam to give them to Bree.

Brad had never let on, but he was a wealthy man because of his stock holdings, most of which were in Kincaid. He hadn't been ready to go to work for the company, but he wasn't about to pass up a great opportunity. So he put as much as he could into the company stock.

For now, though, Adam was content to hold Bree, and she was content to be held while they shared their grief. After the funeral was soon enough to deal with Brad's will.

CHAPTER 1

*M*id July, three years later

Kincaid Holding's headquarters, Adam Kincaid's office

"MR. KINCAID. YOU HAVE A VISITOR." Emily Simmons, Adam's assistant, stood in the office doorway. She wasn't very tall and the door to his office was massive. She looked like a child standing there. Only the laugh lines around her mouth and crinkles at the corners of her eyes gave her away.

His office, a large conference room, and the reception area where Emily worked were the only things on this floor. His office was the largest room. It boasted two leather Queen Anne chairs in front of his desk, which was piled high with reports on a company he was thinking of acquiring. The laptop on the right side of the desk was open to a spreadsheet.

Against the wall to his left was a sitting area with a leather couch and two matching over-stuffed leather chairs. The table in front of the sofa was gleaming chrome with a smoked glass top. On the table was a beautiful Ming vase he'd picked up on his last trip to Hong Kong.

The back wall was entirely glass. The vast windows were tinted dark, so the afternoon sun didn't glare into and heat the room. The wall opposite the sitting area was floor to ceiling bookshelves. The cases were arranged so some were only half shelves. The book-cases held books and more treasures from the Orient. More vases, some very large and some no taller than a paperback book, were artfully arranged on the shelves, intermingling with the leather-bound books.

The carpeting was plush and light gray. It silenced Emily's entrance into his office.

He looked up. "Who is it?"

"A woman named Sally Raines. She says it's of a personal nature."

"I don't know anyone named Sally Raines." Even as he said it, a memory niggled in the back of his mind. He shook his head to rid himself of the thought. "Very well, send her in."

A statuesque blonde woman carrying a baby in a car seat with a diaper bag over the other shoulder entered the room. "Hello, Adam. Long time no see."

He pushed back the leather chair, stood and came around the massive mahogany desk. "I remember you. It's been about a year-and-a-half since we…uh…

connected." He shouldn't be surprised that she found him, but he was.

"Fifteen months to be exact." She set her burdens on the floor, then bent and extracted the baby from the carrier. "I'd like you to meet Lilly. Lilly Kincaid, your daughter."

Adam's eyebrows flew up his forehead, and his eyes popped wide. "My daughter? That's impossible." He looked at the blonde baby with the blue-gray eyes.

The baby looked back at him and graced him with a toothless grin.

He smiled back and then realized what he was doing and frowned.

"Oh, it's very possible. I've got her birth certificate, declaring you as the father, and you can get a DNA test if you want, but she *is* your daughter. And she's the reason I'm here."

He narrowed his eyes. "I suppose you want money." He remembered a wild weekend with Sally, but he'd had people try to shake him down for money before.

Sally smiled. "Nothing of the kind. I'm here to give her to you. I'm tired, and I have an opportunity that I can't have a child for. You have the wherewithal to raise her quite easily. All you have to do is hire someone."

"You can't do this. I don't know the first thing about babies." He ran a hand through his hair as his pulse raced. He couldn't do this. How was he supposed to raise a daughter? "I have some business deals coming up, and I can't be a single father for them." *Danvers will never agree to my offer if I'm a single father.*

She laughed. "Don't be ridiculous. In this day and age, there isn't a stigma to being a single parent."

He rolled his eyes and paced, wrapping a hand around the back of his neck. "You don't understand. This is a very old-fashioned couple, and they're set in their ways. If you have children, you have to be married with two parents."

Sally wasn't moved. "Then I guess you better find a wife."

Adam sighed. "How am I supposed to do that in time? I have a meeting with him in two weeks."

Sally lifted a brow and then shrugged. "That's your problem. Surely, you have a friend or friends with sisters, who wouldn't mind marrying a billionaire."

Adam narrowed his eyes and furrowed his brows. "And *you* don't want money from me? I find that hard to believe."

"Well, believe it. I'm headed to the Middle East for my dream job, and I mean to take it. Now *there* is a place where you can't be a single parent." She closed the distance to Adam and shifted Lilly into his arms. "I have to go. My plane leaves at noon, less than two hours from now, and you know how Denver International Airport is. Or maybe you don't. You probably have a private plane and don't have to go through TSA."

He shrugged. "I don't deal with DIA at all, so I have no idea about TSA other than what I see on the news.

My plane is at Centennial Airport. Are you sure you don't want money? I've never met a woman who didn't want my money."

"I don't. I like to work for what I get. It was the way I was raised, and I hope you'll instill those values in Lilly. Goodbye, Adam. Have a good life." She turned and walked out the door, closing it behind her.

"Wait!" But she was gone. Adam turned his gaze to his daughter. *His daughter.*

She looked up at him with big blue-gray eyes, his eyes, and pounded her fist against his chest.

Adam was thirty-six years old and had younger siblings but hadn't paid much attention to them when they were babies. "What am I going to do with you, little one?" Then a thought struck him. Bree. He could kill two birds with one stone if she agreed to his proposition.

"What will I do if Bree says no?" He didn't know why he was asking Lilly, but it was almost as if she understood because she gave him another toothless grin. "Well, at least your mother left you with a car seat, so we can go see Bree together. I have a feeling that once she sees you, she won't have any qualms about marrying us."

Adam put Lilly into the car seat and then realized he didn't have any idea how to strap her in. He strode to the door, opened it, and saw Emily at her desk. "Emily, can you come in here for a moment, please?"

"Sure."

He held the door open, then closed it behind her.

"I need your help." He pointed at Lilly, sitting in her car seat. "I don't know how to strap her in. Do you? You have children, so I thought you could teach me."

Emily stared at Lilly. She turned toward Adam. "That woman left her baby with you. Why?"

"Apparently, one of my indiscretions had an unintended result."

"I would say so." She moved toward the baby and then lowered herself to her knees. "Hello, sweetheart. Aren't you just the most precious little thing."

Adam watched as Emily secured Lilly into the car seat. He pulled out his phone and made notes of exactly which strap went where.

"What vehicle do you have today?"

"The Jag."

Emily shook her head. "You can't put her in that Jaguar. You'll have to take my Mercedes." She looked up at him. "It's a good thing you pay me well, and I can afford a reliable, four-door vehicle. You always have to make sure you have a back seat in whatever car you drive when you have Lilly." She rose from the floor. "Come on, I'll show you how to buckle her in." Emily turned and walked out of the office, leaving Adam to look after her. "Well, are you coming?" she called from the outer office.

"Yes, we're right behind you." He picked up Lilly and the diaper bag, then followed Emily.

In the summer warmth of the parking garage, Adam followed the woman to her car, a beautiful burgundy Mercedes E550 sedan.

Emily pressed the key fob, went directly to the passenger side back door, and opened it.

"You want to put her in the passenger side if you can, so you can see her in your rear-view mirror. It's just a little more relief to see her as you drive. Let me have her."

Adam passed the baby in the car seat to his assistant.

She deftly wove the seat belt through the car seat frame and tugged it for good measure. "Now, you can get her home. I'll have Eric drop me by your place to pick up my car."

"Oh, don't bother him." He reached into his pocket. "Take the Jag and just exchange cars." He handed her the keys. "And thank you. You went above and beyond today."

She beamed. "All in a day's work at Kincaid Holdings."

Adam laughed. "At least you're not bored. You couldn't have been with me for ten years and been too bored."

"Definitely not." She grinned. "Take care of her. She's precious cargo." She turned to leave and then turned back to him. "Adam what about the Danvers acquisition? How will you care for a baby with all that's happening there?"

"If my plan works, I'll kill two birds with one stone."

"And if it doesn't?"

"I honestly don't know."

He was surprised that he felt so possessive of Lilly

in such a short amount of time. Yet, he realized she was already a part of his life, and he wouldn't let anyone take her from him. "I will. Now that she's mine, I plan on taking the best care of her."

"Will you still have a DNA test?"

He shrugged. "That goes without saying, though at this point I don't know what I'll do if it comes back negative. Her mother's gone to the Middle East for some dream job, and I won't put the baby in foster care. So, she's mine regardless. Besides, my name is on her birth certificate."

She placed a hand on his arm and gazed up at him. "And she has your eyes. You don't get that blue-gray color every day."

He chuckled. "No, you definitely don't. You need to reschedule my afternoon meetings."

"To when do you want them rescheduled?"

"Day after tomorrow."

"Consider it done. What are your plans for the rest of the day?"

"I don't know yet."

"Well, have fun, whatever your plans are."

"Oh, we will. Thank you again."

She waved as she walked back into the building.

"Now, Little Bit, we're going to see someone I hope will want to take on the job of being your mother."

"Baba baba baba." Lilly chattered happily in the back seat.

With each little babble, Adam found his heart growing with what he could only surmise was love. Yet he'd loved no one like he did this newest addition to his family. What was it about babies that affected people this way?

He knew his mother would be thrilled. She'd been after all of her children to get married and give her some grandbabies. Now she would have someone to spoil incessantly.

The drive to Bree's place was relatively stressless. Traffic was pretty good at this time of the morning. He realized he should call to make sure she was home before just stopping by.

He put his phone on the seat beside him and put on the speaker feature. "Call Bree." He heard the phone ring. There was no answer, but that wouldn't stop him. Maybe she was out shopping or perhaps working in the backyard or even listening to music while she wrote. He knew that was how she liked to write and that she didn't answer her phone when she was writing.

He pulled into the driveway of her Cherry Hills Village home. It was the only major purchase she'd made with the money that Brad had left her. And he'd left her a wealthy woman, with hundreds of millions of dollars. She wasn't as rich as Adam...yet, but she was well on her way to being there.

Adam removed Lilly from the backseat and headed to the front door, where he rang the doorbell. He heard the chimes. He was just about to press it again when the door opened.

Bree stood there in shorts, a t-shirt and sneakers.

"Adam, it's so good—what do you have there? A baby? You should come in and get him out of the heat."

"Her. This is Lilly."

"Well come in." She stepped back and waited until he was inside before closing the door behind him.

He stepped into a two-story foyer, where they stood on white marble tile with streaks of gold running through it. He looked up at the chandelier, an antique with small crystal globes for lights. The fixture sparkled like it was covered in diamonds when it was on at night.

"Come into the kitchen and I'll fix us some iced tea." She sniffed the air. "And perhaps give Lilly a new diaper. Do you have diapers? I don't see a diaper bag."

Adam slapped his forehead. "It's in the car. I hope there are diapers and bottles in it. I'll be right back." He set Lilly's carrier on the kitchen table.

When he came back, Bree was holding Lilly. Adam couldn't get over how natural she looked. With her blonde hair and sapphire blue eyes, she could be Lilly's mother. He stood in the entryway and just watched as she talked to Lilly.

She held Lilly on her hip and swayed with her. "What is a sweet baby like you doing with Adam? Hmm?"

He moved forward into the kitchen. The marble tile was continued in this room, and she'd installed black granite countertops with gold streaks running through it, too. The kitchen had all black appliances including stove with double ovens, refrigerator, dishwasher, trash compactor and microwave.

Her cabinets were oak with glass in the doors on the upper ones and solid oak on the lower cabinets.

"You two appear to be getting along famously, although Lilly looks like she's about to make a meal of your hair."

Bree laughed and tugged the baby's fist out of her long hair.

Her hair was one of the things Adam loved about Bree. She had golden-blonde hair that flowed in waves and curls to the middle of her back. She liked to wear it loose, though when she worked in the garden, she pulled it up into a messy bun on top of her head, like it was now.

"Shall we see what's in the diaper bag and then while I change her, you can tell me her story."

Bree had moved the car seat to the floor and put some towels on the table.

"If you spread these out, then we can get this done quickly. You don't know how to change her diaper, do you?"

"No. I know nothing about babies."

"Then you better watch and learn. Where is her mother?"

"Gone. Lilly's my daughter."

"It thought so. She has your eyes, you know." Then she grinned and placed her hand on his arm. "I still can't believe you're a father. You're thirty-six and I figured if you weren't married again by now, you wouldn't be. And I never thought you'd have children. This is monumental, Adam."

Adam shrugged as he finished spreading the towels on the table. "I never thought this would happen. I've always been careful. I guess I had a faulty condom."

"I guess so. It happens to the best." Bree laid Lilly on the towels, removed her onesie and took off the soaked diaper. "I need the wipes."

He found the tub of baby wipes and handed her one.

She washed Lilly and then put a dry diaper on her along with a clean onesie.

Adam watched closely, taking notes on his phone. It didn't seem to be hard, but he knew that this was just a wet diaper, and she would have a messy one sometime soon.

Taking Lilly back into her arms, Bree handed her to Adam.

"So, tell me how you ended up with a daughter, and why now?"

He told her the entire story, leaving nothing out.

"Well, that's quite a tale. Let me get us some iced tea, and you can tell me why you're here. Not that I don't love seeing you, but this is fairly strange you have to admit."

Bree walked to the refrigerator.

The large kitchen had an eating area where Adam sat at the round oak table. He held Lilly in his lap.

She pounded on the table with her little fists and babbled happily.

"I'm here because I need your help and not just with Lilly. I need a wife and Lilly needs a mother."

Bree's hands stilled as she reached for the pitcher of tea. "Why did you come to me? Do you want me to help you find a wife?"

Adam shook his head. "No. I want you to *be* my wife." He hurried on before she could speak. "Please hear me out before you say no."

She continued with her task and came to the table with two large glasses of iced tea. She made it with just a little sugar, just enough to cut the bitterness tea sometimes had, but not make it sweet.

Her mother had always prepared it that way, and Bree continued with the tradition. He found he preferred it served this way.

"I need a wife for a deal I'm working on. The couple who own the company are rather old-fashioned and very rigid about it. They want whoever they choose to go with, to be a family man. Now, especially with Lilly, I need a wife." He hurried on. "It wouldn't have to be permanent. A marriage of convenience. Please say you'll do it." *She has to say yes. I won't get the Breckenridge account if I don't have Danvers first.*

Bree was quiet for a bit. She sipped her tea. "I'll get attached to Lilly. I never wanted to marry. Not after Brad. You know that. And I thought you would never marry again after Valerie."

His gut churned, and he stiffened at the mention of his ex-wife. "I know. I'm sorry. I never should have asked you. Don't worry about it, I'll figure out something else. I—"

She placed her glass on the table and smiled at Lilly.

The baby started giggling as if she knew the funniest joke.

Bree turned her gaze back to Adam. "I'll do it. I want to be a mother, Adam but I don't want our friendship to become romantic. I want to be loved, as a woman, before I have sex with anyone, including you. You're my best friend; so of course, I'll help you. I'm twenty-eight and this will be my only chance to have a child. When would you want to get married?"

Adam let out the breath he hadn't known he was holding. "As soon as possible. Unless you want a big church wedding, I thought we could just do it at the house with a justice of the peace."

She waved a hand and smiled. "That's fine. I don't want a big wedding. That was my dream when I thought I was marrying Brad; I don't need or want that anymore."

"Today is Wednesday. Is Saturday too soon?"

She shook her head. "That will be fine. What will you do with Lilly until you get her some furniture?"

"She'll just sleep with me. I thought I'd go furniture shopping after leaving here. Unless…do you want to go with me to pick out the furniture? You know more about what she'll need than I do."

She grinned. "I'd love to go with you. We'll purchase a portable playpen you can take home tonight and let her sleep in that."

Adam nodded. "That's a great idea. What else will she need?" He pulled out his phone and started taking notes again. He was making a lot of notes, he realized. Having a child was a lot harder than he expected.

She put an index finger on her chin and pursed her lips. "Well, are you planning on doing a complete nursery?"

"Of course. I'll turn the bedroom closest to mine into a nursery. You can have the bedroom on the other side so if she needs anything one of us will surely hear her. Although, we haven't talked about it, I assume you'll be moving into my house."

"Of course. I want to be there at night if Lilly needs me. Besides, you'll still have to travel. You can't put your business on hold, and I'll be there for when you can't be."

He nodded, and then his phone chirped. He pulled it out of a front pocket in his pants and looked at it. "I need to take this. Afterward we can talk about furniture."

"I'll make a list of what she'll need while you take your call."

Adam walked out of the kitchen to the hall to the living room. "Kincaid."

He listened. "I don't care what they want. I'm not selling the land. I have my own plans for that property. Tell them I'll discuss those with them when I return to the office. I'm taking the rest of this week off. I plan on returning to the office next week."

He listened again. "Thanks, Emily. If anyone calls,

take a message. I'll return their calls when I get back to the office."

"Yes, thank you. Goodbye." He shoved the phone back in his pocket and returned to Bree. He sat across from her, picked up his tea and took a calming sip.. "Now, the furniture. What does she need?"

Bree picked up the list she'd made and read from it. "You'll want to buy a crib, the playpen, a chest of drawers, and two changing tables, one for the nursery and one for the main floor. You'll need a nightstand and lamp with a night light. It would probably be a good idea to get a music box to play while she settles down and goes to sleep."

Adam's stomach turned at the thought of all the things a baby needed. "I'm thankful you agreed to help me because I can make copious notes about what she needs but I'll never know what to get if there are choices. Besides, I don't know where to get all this stuff."

She chuckled. "That's just the furniture. She'll also need diapers and clothes."

"What kind of diapers and clothes? What clothes does a baby wear?"

Bree appeared to take pity on him. "Come on. We're going to my friend's baby boutique. She'll have everything you need." Bree reached out and touched his arm. "Trust me."

"I aways do," he replied honestly. She was his best friend. He trusted her with his life and now, more importantly, with Lilly's.

*B*ree placed Lilly into her car seat and then grabbed her purse from the breakfast bar. "I've got her, you just open the car, and I'll get her strapped in and we can go." *Adam is so clueless. He really does need me.*

"Gotcha." Adam hurried through the front door to the Mercedes in the driveway.

Bree followed at a slower pace because she had Lilly. "Nice car. I didn't know you had a Mercedes. Except for the Lincoln Navigator, I thought all your vehicles were of the fast variety."

Adam held the passenger side back door open.

She placed the car seat down and wove the seat belt through the bottom of the equipment, pulling hard to make sure it was secure. Then she stepped back and Adam closed the door.

"I don't. You're right I tend to like fast and sleek. The Mercedes is a great car and now that I have Lilly, I might buy one. This one belongs to Emily. I drove the Jag today."

She held up her hand and chuckled. "You don't have to say more. I think you'll find that with Lilly along you'll be getting a lot more use from your Navigator."

He ran a hand behind his neck. "Yeah. It will take some adjusting to accommodate the little sweetheart."

Bree slid into the passenger's side seat.

Adam pulled her seatbelt out and handed it to her.

She looked up at him and smiled. "Thanks."

He grinned. "Anytime." Adam walked around the front of the car, slipped behind the wheel, and buckled up before starting the engine. "So where is this store?"

* * *

IT TOOK them about twenty minutes to get to their destination. The boutique was located in downtown Denver on the 16th Street Mall. It was on the corner of 16th Street and Curtis. The two store fronts showed baby clothes and a gorgeous wicker bassinet.

After they entered the store, Bree checked to see if her friend was working. She was not, so Bree helped him pick out all the furniture and the diapers. When she took him to the clothes area, she picked up the onesies, t-shirts, bibs and little shorts, including swim panties. She picked up a couple of different sizes because she knew from her experience with her siblings how fast babies grow. She also got some footie pajamas that were just a little heavier material than the onesies and would keep Lilly warm without being too hot.

Adam was transfixed by the little pink dresses with ruffles. Then he saw tiny panties with ruffles and had to have those, too.

Bree giggled as he put several of every size and color dress and panties into the cart.

They included a mobile of zebras for over her crib and several soft toys she could hold on to and chew on if she wanted.

Bree picked out the portable playpen, sheets, and a couple of blankets for both the playpen and the crib. She even found a ballerina music box that played Brahms Lullaby.

All these things for a little human were pocket change for Adam, but delivery was free, and most importantly, it included set-up. This alone was worth more than the furniture and clothes for Lilly. Adam was not mechanically inclined, after all.

They walked out, with Bree holding Lilly.

Adam loaded the bags of clothes, toys, and the playpen into the trunk.

"Do you want to come to the house and help me get her settled? She'll have to stay in my room until the nursery is ready."

Lilly began to fuss.

"Yeah, we better get to your house so she can eat. It's been a long time since I met her, and you've had her even longer. She's been a wonderful baby, so easy going, but she's got to be hungry." Bree placed the baby in the car seat and strapped her in. Then she settled into the passenger seat and buckled up.

Adam slid behind the wheel and put on his seatbelt before starting the car.

"What do I feed her? Do I need to get baby food first? I'll have to let Carole know so she can pick some up and keep it on hand. She's the best housekeeper in the world and she has kids and now a grandchild. She'll know what I need."

Bree shook her head. "Carole is the best house-keeper in the world. I even thought about trying to steal her from you, but for our immediate needs, I saw some bottles and formula in the diaper bag. When we get to your house, I'll show you how to make it."

While he drove, Adam glanced at Bree. She had a smile on her face and looked beautiful. Serene.

"How do you know so much about babies?"

"I was the oldest of six children. I started taking care of babies when I was eight and it's not something you forget how to do. Besides I've always wanted children. That's why I agreed to marry you. I want more than anything to be Lilly's mother. She's such a sweet baby."

They arrived at Adam's home. It wasn't far from Bree's house, though he had a house on several acres of land in the middle of Cherry Hills.

His house was a stately colonial style with a large, covered porch, including white columns supporting the roof.

He punched in the security code, and the gate

swung open. The driveway wound around the house to the six-car garage in the back.

"If you'll get Lilly, I'll get the rest of this stuff." She'd visited his home frequently and was familiar with the layout.

"Okay." Bree released her seatbelt and exited the car. Then she lifted Lilly, in her car seat, out of the vehicle and headed to the door to the kitchen.

Adam carried all the bags in one trip, then the diapers and playpen on the second trip. He stacked all the bags on one end of the cherry wood kitchen table. His kitchen was quite spacious. He'd designed it so the kitchen and family room were basically one big room. That's the way his parent's home had been. He liked it, so designed this house just like theirs but on a grander scale. He carried the playpen through the kitchen, down the hall, past the formal dining room and his office, to the left one of the two staircases, and leaned it against the first stair.

When he returned, he heard Lilly crying. She was in her car seat on the opposite end of the table from the bags of baby clothes, sheets, and blankets were behind her.

Bree was getting a bottle ready.

He turned to Bree. "What do I do?"

"Come here and learn how to make a bottle. She'll be fine for a moment."

Adam walked over to Bree with his phone out.

She placed warm water in the bottle, then added the formula. Covering the tip of the nipple with an index finger, she shook it until all the formula was mixed with the water. "There you go. Now, pick her up and try to calm her. She's just hungry. And now you can feed her."

"Me! I don't know how to—"

"You're about to learn. Go sit with her on the family room sofa and I'll bring you the bottle."

He needed to learn how to do everything for his daughter. He would approach this just like a business takeover. He'd do research, in this case, watching Bree as she interacted with the baby, and then he would do it on his own. He put his phone in his pocket, picked Lilly up from the car seat, and leaned her against his shoulder, patting her back as he walked over to the sofa.

The family room furniture, including the two sofas and two recliners, was covered in a cream-colored, soft fur like material. There was a large screen TV over the river rock fireplace.

He sat down with Lilly, keeping her on his shoulder and patting her back. He was doing his best to calm her and maybe himself, too.

Adam could hire a nanny to take care of her, but he didn't want that for Lilly. It would be a lot easier if he did, but he wanted either him or Bree to be responsible for their daughter.

That thought made him smile. *Their daughter.* She was already in place in both of their hearts. He knew he would fight to the death to keep her safe and thought Bree felt the same way.

She approached with a bottle. "Okay, lay her back on your arm, so her head is nestled in the crook of your arm, so you can feed her. Like this." Bree positioned her arms like she was holding the baby to feed her.

He did as she asked, looking down at Lilly.

Her face was screwed up, tears running down her cheeks as she cried pitifully.

Adam didn't know what to do to help her.

Bree handed him the bottle. "This is what she wants."

He accepted it.

Lilly immediately reached for it and was practically shoving it in her mouth before he could tilt it toward her. Then she settled in and drank, alternately holding the bottle and grabbing Adam's shirt in her little fist.

Bree sat at the other end of the sofa and watched him with Lilly.

The more she drank, the more her eyes closed.

Adam looked over at Bree. "She's going to sleep. Should I let her or keep her awake?"

"If she wants to sleep and stops drinking, then you can burp her and put her to bed. I'll get the playpen ready."

"Okay." He looked up from where Lilly lay in his arms. "Thank you, Bree. I don't know what I would do without you."

"You'd be in a world of hurt, my friend." Then she laughed, grabbed the sheets and blankets before heading out to retrieve the playpen.

Fifteen minutes later, she quietly entered the room. Lilly was asleep.

"Did you burp her?" asked Bree.

Adam shook his head. "I don't know how. I just now took the bottle out of her mouth. She had quit drinking…for the most part. She would stop and every time I tried to remove the bottle, she'd start sucking again."

"For the most part, that's a reflex action. She's not really still hungry but isn't willing to not have something to suck on…when she wants it, of course." Bree retrieved a dish towel from the kitchen, placed it over her shoulder, and plucked Lilly from Adam's arms. "This is how to burp her."

The baby barely awoke, even as Bree placed her against her shoulder and thumped her back.

After she'd burped Lilly, Bree handed the still sleeping baby back to Adam. Then she picked a pacifier from one of the bags, washed it and gave it to Lilly.

The baby took it immediately, even in sleep.

"The pacifier will give her something to suck on and then she won't drink more formula than she needs and give herself a belly ache."

He held his arms, so Lilly was laying on her back and making little snuffle sounds. It was so dang cute he couldn't help but smile as he watched her.

"Let's take her upstairs and lay her down. Then you can ask Carole to keep an eye on her while you take me home. I'll come back with my car and an at least an overnight bag." She grinned. "I won't leave you alone to take care of her tonight. That wouldn't be good for Lilly."

He easily stood, even with Lilly in his arms. "Will you grab a couple of those bags and bring them upstairs? Or would you rather carry her, and I'll get the bags?"

"No, you take her. You need to spend as much time as you can with Lilly, so you feel comfortable caring for her. I'll be here, too, but I think you need to bond with her."

Adam looked down at the sleeping child, ran his palm lightly over her silky blonde hair. "I think I'm already bonded." He suddenly looked up at Bree. "How could Sally just abandon her?"

Bree shrugged. "I can't give you an answer. I couldn't have done it. No matter what the job. I can't imagine any circumstance that would let me abandon my child. Although, selfishly, I'm glad that she did. She's allowing me to have my dream. I'll be a mother, and that's all I've ever wanted to be."

As he looked at her, his brows very slightly furrowed. "Do you wish you and Brad had children?"

"Yes…and…no. I wanted to be married before I had children and then when Brad died, I didn't think I would ever want anything again. Not love or mother-hood or anything. I believe that everything comes to us in its own time, and this is the time I'm supposed to be a mother. Marrying you is my means to an end."

"I understand that. I'm just glad you are helping me, whatever your reasons." He stopped and looked down at her before touching her shoulder, hoping to convey sympathy. "You deserve to be happy, Bree."

She ducked her chin. "I tell myself that, but it's hard. It gets easier every day to go on, but I still mourn. I probably always will."

His heart hurt, thinking about Brad. "It's okay. I miss him, too."

She nodded. "Let's get this sleepy baby upstairs and to bed. Then you'll have to find Carole before we can leave."

Bree had set up the playpen with sheets and blankets. They got Lilly settled into it and then walked downstairs.

Carole was entering the kitchen from the backyard. She carried a basket full of vegetables she'd just harvested from her garden.

Bree and Carole were alike in that they both loved to garden and since Carole and her husband lived in a condominium, she kept a garden at Adam's house.

"Well, you're home early." The trim, middle-aged woman with dark blonde hair smiled at Bree. "How are you, hon? We haven't seen you for a while."

Bree shrugged. "I'm good. Adam needs to ask a favor."

Carole turned her gaze on Adam. "Anything, Boss. What do you need?"

Adam took a deep breath. "I have a sleeping baby upstairs in my room, and I wondered if you would keep an ear open for her while we're gone for a little bit. I need to take Bree home so she can get her car."

Carole's moss green eyes widened. "A baby? Since when do you have a baby?"

Adam ran a hand around the back of his neck. "Since this morning. I'll explain everything when we return. Will you do it?"

"Of course. I might have to go upstairs just to see him."

"Lilly," said Adam. "She's Lilly Kincaid, and she's, my daughter."

Bree hadn't thought Carole's eyes could get any wider. She'd been mistaken. The woman looked like one of those pictures of the children with eyes so big they covered half their face.

"Carole?" Adam waved his hand in front of her face. "Are you okay?"

She shook her head a little and closed her eyes. "Yes. I'm fine. Just very surprised. You couldn't shock me more if you told me, you and Bree were getting married."

"Well, that's good...because we are." He looked over at Bree, then he looked out the door to the backyard. He saw the sixty foot lap pool he'd put in to keep in shape. It was surrounded by lawn. The pool house was in the middle of the length of the pool and was also in the colonial style to match the house.

Directly out the door was a twenty-foot-wide covered patio that ran the length of the house. They could have the ceremony there...if Bree agreed. "I was thinking we could have a small ceremony here in the backyard. We can tell everyone to bring their swimsuits and dress casually. We'll have a pool party for a reception. What do you think?"

Bree was silent for a moment.

Adam frowned, and his chest was tight. He was sure she hated the idea. If she did, what did that bode for their future? Would they be at odds with everything?

She suddenly grinned. "I think that's a perfect idea for this wedding. You've got the patio we can get married on and lots of grass for our family and friends to sit. Then we can change into our bathing suits and go for a swim. I'm glad you bought a couple of those swim panties for Lilly. I get the feeling she'll love the water…just like her daddy."

The tightness in his chest disappeared. Adam grinned and puffed out his chest. "That would be terrific. I plan on teaching her to swim as soon as possible. I heard classes are offered just for babies."

Bree laughed. "They are. You're so funny though. We'll go together and learn all we can so we can continue to teach her here at home, since this is going to be my home now."

He slung an arm around her shoulders as he had since Brad's death. "Let's get this show on the road. I want to be back before she wakes up."

She placed an arm around his waist and headed for the garage. "Do you want to drop the Mercedes by the office and pick up that Jag?"

"And deprive Emily of the treat of driving the Jag? No way."

Bree chuckled.

Adam loved hearing her and grinned, happier than he'd been in a long time. He directed her to the passenger's side and held her seatbelt as she settled in.

"Thanks. You know you don't have to do that. I can pull out my seatbelt."

"I know, but this makes it easier. I'm all about making things easier for you. You're doing me an enormous favor and upending your life in the process."

After he was behind the wheel, she spoke. "First off, I'm not doing you a favor, I'm doing *me* a favor. Second, I gave you my reasons. Though I want to help, I'm not sure I'd saddle myself for life to help you. Lilly is the clencher. Third, don't expect me to give up that little girl for anything. She's mine now, just as much as she's yours." Her voice softened. "I already love her. How can that happen so quickly? How can I have fallen so completely in love with her in the matter of a few hours?"

He opened the gate and then drove toward South University Boulevard. "I don't know, but the same thing has happened to me. She's just special, I guess. I'd give my life for her and, as you said, it's only been a few hours."

He pulled into Bree's driveway.

"You don't have to stay. I'll be over after I've packed a bag."

"All right. Will I need to change her diaper when she wakes?" The thought made him distinctly uncomfortable.

"More than likely. She'll probably sleep for a couple

of hours, though. Babies tend to sleep a lot. And I should be back before she wakes." She unbuckled her seatbelt and opened the car door. "I'll see you soon."

"We'll be waiting."

Bree closed the car door and walked toward the house.

Adam waited until she was inside before leaving. Then he headed back to his home and the little one who'd stolen his heart.

CHAPTER 3

Bree pulled a large suitcase from out of the closet in one of the guest rooms. She walked to her room and opened the walk-in closet. Her clothes were hung by style and then by color to make choosing her outfits easier. Shoe racks held more than fifty pairs of shoes because she had a bit of an obsession with shoes. She packed enough clothes for a week.

From there she headed to her bathroom. She'd had it designed for two people even though she never intended to marry. The shower had two shower heads. The jacuzzi tub was extra-large. She had two sinks in the white marble vanity. She packed her toiletries and makeup into a large, train-case-style makeup case and placed it in the suitcase.

Next, she went to her office and picked up her laptop. She had a book to finish and a deadline to meet. Even though it was a self-imposed deadline, she would like to meet it, nonetheless.

Laying on her desk were also three books, one by Amanda M. Lee, one by Lily Harper Hart and one by Jana Deleon. They were all cozy mysteries, which she loved. She always wished she could write those, but they weren't her forte. She wrote contemporary romance and was perfectly happy doing so. She picked those up, too, and packed them in her laptop bag. She wasn't sure she would get much reading done, but she liked to read before bed and was prepared.

Once she was finished, she checked the doors and windows to make sure they were locked and went through the kitchen to the garage.

She owned a Ford F150 truck. She'd opted for the truck when she started working in her garden and needed to transport plants and soil. Her garden was on the sprinkler system with drip irrigation. She'd harvested everything up to that point. The vegetables left wouldn't become ripe for another two weeks or so and she would have to get Adam to give her time to harvest them.

Once she was done with the garden project, she'd decided she liked the truck and kept it. She also had a Dodge Charger, but she didn't drive it that often, preferring the truck.

Bree texted Adam to let him know she was on her way. She had some trepidation about moving into the home of Brad's best friend, but she reminded herself that Adam was her best friend, too.

She already knew the code for the gate, since she was a regular visitor to Adam's home. It hadn't taken long to drive over there, and he was waiting for her when she pulled in front of the house.

She lowered the window when he walked up to the truck. "What's up?"

"There is room in the garage." He handed her an opener. "If you need it, the code is 1719. Just pull in and park in the empty space. I'm moving the Jag to the storage garage when Emily returns it."

"Are you sure? I don't mind parking the truck in the driveway."

He shook his head and leaned against the door. "I'm sure. I want you to be comfortable here and that includes parking in the garage."

Bree took the garage door opener and pressed the button. The door right in front of her, closest to the kitchen, opened.

"This is great. Thank you."

Adam reached in and squeezed her left hand. "Bree, I don't know what I'd do if you weren't helping me. I can never thank you enough."

She gazed down at his hand on her hand, and a sense of warmth flowed through her. "Well, good, because you'll have to help me now."

"Anything. What can I do?"

"Let me park and get my stuff inside, then we'll talk."

"Sounds like a plan." He gave her hand another squeeze and backed away from the vehicle.

She pulled in and parked. His six-car garage was wider than normal, so she had plenty of room on either side of her truck when it was parked. It was also deeper than hers because there was plenty of room to walk around the front and the back of the vehicle when it was parked correctly.

She exited the vehicle and opened the back door to get her suitcase and laptop.

"Here, I'll get that." Adam reached inside the truck, pulling out her luggage and shutting the door behind him. "Come on in. Lilly is still sleeping…or she was last time I checked."

Bree chuckled as she walked beside him. "How many times have you been up there?"

He shrugged sheepishly. "Just three."

"Three! I've only been gone for about forty-five minutes. I told you she'd sleep for two hours. Give the kid a break." She gave him the side-eye. "You're going to be one of those fathers who checks every time she goes to sleep to see if she's still breathing, aren't you?"

Adam didn't meet her gaze, but he walked through the kitchen to the foyer and up the stairs. "Let's get you settled."

Bree couldn't help but smile at his gruff countenance as she followed him upstairs.

He stopped at the first door on the right. "This will be your room. I hope you find it comfortable. If you want anything changed, just let me know and I'll make it happen.

"I'm sure it will be fine. After all I'm the one who helped you decorate this house, remember?"

"I remember. I just want you to be comfortable.

Change anything you like in the house. It's been a couple of years since you decorated, so knock yourself out updating it."

"I'll consider it. I've been thinking though, I'd like the second master across from yours. It's bigger and I need some room to spread out. A room that is just mine and I'll still be close enough to hear Lilly if she needs me."

He snapped his fingers. "Good idea. I should have thought of it."

"You can't be expected to think of everything." She laid a hand on his free arm. Again, the warmth of his body passed through her. "This is a new situation for both of us. We need to be gentle with each other, as well as with Lilly."

"You're right. I'm just not used to living with some-one." He walked up to the bedroom across from his. The master bedrooms were very large, over one thou-sand square feet each. Between the two of them, they occupied half of the second floor. Each one included a full, private bath with an extra-large Jacuzzi tub, double walk-in closets, and a fireplace which separated the sitting room from the bedroom but whose flames could be seen in both. This room differed from Adam's in that his was done in brown for the curtains and bedspread with cream walls and brown trim. The carpet was Berber wool and was very thick and plush.

· · ·

HER ROOM WAS DONE in shades of blue. Dark blue in the curtains, bedspread and trim. The walls were light blue with dark blue trim and thick, pale blue carpet.

Bree walked into the room after Adam. "Yes, this is much better. I like having space that is just mine." She hadn't seen the room since she'd decorated it. The furniture was the same. Whereas Adam's room was decorated with dark mahogany, as was his preference, she'd picked light oak furniture for this room. The sleigh bed was one of her favorite pieces. She'd picked a large bureau with a mirror and eight drawers. The Tall Boy chest and end tables with a drawer on top and double doors below matched the finish on the bed. Large table lamps were on the end tables rather than the much smaller bedroom lamps most rooms featured. This room also had double walk-in closets with more than enough room for all her clothes and accessories.

Adam's mouth turned down and his forehead furrowed. "I'm sorry, Bree. I should have realized and never offered you the guest room. I don't know what I was thinking."

She waved off the apology. "Don't worry about it. We've got it straightened out."

"Well, I'll leave you to unpack. If you need anything, let me know."

"I will. I'll just put this stuff away and then meet you in the kitchen...after checking on Lilly, of course. We should probably put her to sleep where we are rather than alone in your room, at least when we're not up here. We'll get a baby monitor and won't have to worry about that, but we'll still need the playpen downstairs so she can be safe while she's down there. We don't want to hold her all the time. I should have thought of that when we were at the boutique."

"Regardless, I'll work some from home. Emily can handle any of the day-to-day stuff and I won't have to go in except for meetings, but I do have a lot of those. I want to be as hands on with Lilly as possible."

Bree nodded and clasped her hands behind her. "I understand. I feel the same way. I don't want her to be raised by babysitters and nannies. I normally work from home anyway, so she can be with one of us all the time."

"Those are my thoughts exactly. After Lilly wakes up, I'll take the playpen downstairs. We can turn the library into your office. Would you mind sharing mine until that happens?"

"Not at all. I can write anywhere, really. But I would like to bring my desktop over. I can use the laptop, but I prefer the big computer."

Adam nodded. "Understood. Well, I'll see you in a short while." He made his way to the door and went out.

Bree placed the suitcase on the bed. She wanted to unpack it as soon as possible so the clothes didn't get too wrinkled.

She'd packed a couple pairs of jeans, t-shirts, black dress pants, two silk blouses, and a swimsuit, one of her more modest one-piece suits. The garment was single shouldered and showed off her figure, which wasn't too bad. She also brought a bikini and a floral print skirt coverup that went with either suit.

She brought a nice pink silk sheath with matching shoes she could get married in. Nothing too fancy. She didn't want that, but still not jeans, either.

When she was finished unpacking, she walked across the hall to check on Lilly.

Bree found the baby awake, chewing her right fist and playing with her left foot. "Well, hello, sweetheart. How long have you been awake? I bet you need a fresh diaper, huh?" She walked into the bathroom and got a bath towel. When she returned to the bedroom, she laid the towel on Adam's bed, folded in half for extra protection. She picked up the diaper bag off the floor by the bed. Then she bent and swept the baby into her arms and headed down to the kitchen.

She didn't immediately find Adam, so she put a baby blanket on the floor. From the diaper bag, she pulled out a diaper, the wipes and the A&D Ointment. She placed all of them to the side of the blanket. Then she laid Lilly on the blanket while she prepared a bottle. By the time she was finished, she saw that the baby had rolled over and was doing a turtle walk across the Moroccan tile floor.

"Well, aren't you so smart? I've not had a baby belly crawling at six months before. Usually, my brothers and sisters waited at least another month. Yes." She tickled Lilly's stomach. "You are just so smart. We definitely can't just leave you on the bed alone, you'll roll right off."

"Who'll roll right off what?" Adam strolled in from the garage.

Bree looked up as Adam entered. "Lilly can't be left alone on a bed. She's rolling and trying to crawl. She'll roll off the bed if we don't watch her. So, if you have to put her down for any reason, lay her on the floor on her back and preferably not near the bed. She's liable to roll right under it."

Adam raised his eyebrows. "Good to know." He walked over and squatted next to Lilly. "So, little bit, you've been giving your mommy something new to worry about. Taking care of you will be quite the experience for your old dad. But I'll learn. Nothing will stop me from being the best dad ever."

Bree chuckled. "You are going to be the best dad. I have no doubt about that because you love her so much. However, now she needs changing and she's probably hungry. Do you want to change her while I finish getting a bottle ready...just in case?"

He looked up, eyes wide. Then he swallowed hard. "Well, I need to get good at this, so yeah, I'll change her. You have everything ready, so here goes." Adam took off the used diaper, cleaned her gently and put the new diaper on...backwards.

Laughing, Bree set the bottle on the table and pointed at the diaper. "That wasn't bad except you need to put it on the other way around." She opened the tapes, turned the diaper around and snugged it up around her belly with the tapes..

Adam took notes on his phone. "Ah, that would make it easier."

"Immensely, now let's see if she's hungry.""

"Okay." He picked up the baby and walked to the sofa in the family room off the kitchen. The room held two sofas, one on the long side of the room. A gas fireplace on the third wall and a large screen TV above the fireplace. Two recliners faced the TV with their backs to the kitchen.

A large round table was between the kitchen and the family room. The three spaces were open to each other, making one big room.

Bree handed him the bottle, then bent and adjusted Lilly in his arms by bringing her head up a bit.

When Adam put the nipple up to Lilly's mouth, she turned her head. He tried again with the same result. "Am I doing something wrong?"

"Nope, she's just not hungry. Since it's nice outside, how about we get changed and get her into her swim pants and get her used to the water. That will make it easier when she actually takes lessons."

"Sounds good. I have to call the office first, but I'll be out in about twenty minutes."

He didn't sound thrilled at the prospect, so she took pity on him and nodded. "I'll change her after I get on my suit. Let me have her."

Adam passed the baby to Bree. "Thanks. I think I can only learn so much in one day."

Bree chuckled. *We'll see how much you can learn. I bet. it's more than you believe it is.*

＊ ＊ ＊

SATURDAY ARRIVED WAY TOO SOON, but Bree was ready to get it over with. The wedding was on the back patio. It was big enough to hold all the attendees so they could be out of the sun.

She stood in the nursery with Adam and Lilly.

"Is everyone here?" Adam picked up Lilly from her crib.

All the furniture had been delivered and set up in the nursery. They kept the playpen downstairs to let her play in.

Bree was happier than she thought she would be. She really hadn't wanted to marry, but she couldn't turn down the chance to live her dream. "Yes, everyone we love is here. All your brothers, your sister, my two sisters and three brothers. Our parents and Emily and her husband. And, of course, Carole and her husband. What time will the justice of the peace be here?"

"He should be here now. Let's go downstairs and see if everything is set up. I'm sure it is. Carole is nothing if not efficient."

Bree smoothed her hands over her dress. "Are you ready?" Adam looked very handsome in a blue pinstripe suit with a pink shirt and tie.

Adam was looking at her. "You look beautiful. I

can't believe you're going to marry me...of your own free will."

She laughed. "Of course, I am. We both want something that we can only get together. So, let's go do this and get to the reception or should I say barbeque. I'm so glad you agreed to keep it simple."

"I want you to be happy and if this makes you happy then it does me, too."

They walked down to the formal living room off the foyer. The room wasn't one of Bree's favorites, but in a house this size, over seven thousand square feet, she supposed it was necessary.

The justice of the peace, a friend of Adam's, was waiting with his wife. He stepped forward to greet them.

"Adam." He looked over at Bree. "And you are the lovely bride-to-be. I'm James Coughlin and this is my wife, Rose."

Bree held out her right hand.

James, who was as tall as Adam, with gorgeous silver hair, shook it.

Then she shook hands with Rose.

"You two make just the cutest couple. And that little munchkin is charming. May I hold her?" asked Rose, a petite woman of about fifty with beautiful auburn hair. Whether it was dyed, Bree couldn't tell, but if it was, they did a fantastic job.

"Of course," Adam passed Lilly to Rose.

"Hello, little darlin'. How are you today? Your

mommy and daddy are getting married today, do you know that? Hmm?"

Of course, Lilly didn't answer. Instead, she watched Rose with wide blue eyes and then stuffed her left fist in her mouth.

Bree had dressed her in one of the frilly pink dresses and matching rubber panties and pulled her hair up to the top of her head in a little ponytail, just like Pebbles Flintstone. She looked absolutely adorable.

Adam watched them for a moment and then turned to James. "Are you ready to get this show on the road? I think everyone has arrived and is waiting for us outside."

"I am. Rose, give the baby back and let's get you seated," said James.

Rose frowned and started to turn away, but then smiled and handed Lilly to Bree. "Are you holding her during the ceremony?"

Bree nodded as she accepted Lilly. "I am. She's as much a part of this as anyone and we want her with us."

The older woman clasped her hands in front of her. "I think that's wonderful. I'm glad to see you taking this wedding seriously."

"We are definitely serious," said Adam. "This is a fresh start for all of us."

Bree nodded. "Most definitely." She'd arranged to have all of her clothes and personal items moved to Adam's in the last three days. She was ready to begin her new life.

Adam led the way out to the backyard. Along the back of the house was a large, covered patio. Farther out was an outdoor pool and pool house. On the other side of the pool house was Carole's vegetable garden and beyond that was a couple of acres of manicured lawn.

Bree wondered how he'd feel if she took over part of the yard for a garden. She loved her flowers.

As soon as they walked out, everyone seated began to clap.

Smiling, Bree waved to the crowd and took Lilly's hand and waved it, too.

The JP took his place at the west edge of the patio.

Adam had ordered a bower of flowers for him and Bree to stand under while taking their vows. They walked there and stood facing each other.

James began the ceremony. "Dearly beloved, we are gathered here to unite this man and this woman in holy matrimony. Before we start, is there anyone present who knows why these two should not be wed?" He gazed at the gathering and waited for two beats. "Very well. Do you Adam Sean Kincaid, take this woman, Brianna Aurora Taylor, to be your lawfully wedded wife? To have and to hold, through sickness and in health, for richer and for poorer, for as long as you both shall live?"

"I do." Adam's voice rang out loud and clear.

Bree hoped hers would be as strong.

The JP turned toward her. "Do you, Brianna Aurora Taylor, take this man, Adam Sean Kincaid, to be your lawfully wedded husband? To have and to hold, through sickness and in health, for richer and for poorer, for as long as you both shall live?"

Bree gazed up at Adam and then at Lilly and smiled. "I do."

"Do you have rings to exchange?" asked James.

"We do." Bree and Adam said in unison.

"Very well. Adam, repeat after me. With this ring, I thee wed."

Adam removed her ring from his right little finger and smiled as he held her left hand. "With this ring, I thee wed." He slipped the platinum band that was covered with ten perfectly round ¼ carat diamonds onto the third finger.

Bree lifted her hand and gazed at the ring. She knew it was coming, had even helped him pick it out, but seeing it was still a jolt to her heart. She always believed Brad would be placing the wedding band on her finger. Tears pricked the back of her eyes, but she blinked them away and smiled at Adam and passed Lilly to him.

He held her with his right arm.

Justice James smiled. "Repeat after me. With this ring, I thee wed."

She removed Adam's ring from her right thumb and then gazed up at Adam while she held his left hand. He hadn't wanted anything gaudy, but she'd talked him into this ring. The band had one large two carat center diamond, surrounded by four ¼ carat diamonds. The metal was platinum. "With this ring, I thee wed." She grinned.

The justice smiled and clasped his hands over his stomach. "By the power vested in me by the State of Colorado, the County of Arapahoe and the City of Cherry Hills Village, I now pronounce you husband and wife. You may kiss the bride."

Adam smiled and leaned down. He gave Bree a soft kiss on the mouth, then smiled widely and turned to the attendees. He moved Lilly to his left arm and grabbed Bree's left hand with his right one. Then he raised them both up, just like when a fighter wins a match.

The crowd broke into applause and whistles as Bree and Adam moved from the patio to the grass where everyone was seated and down the aisle between the chairs.

The sound startled Lilly, and she whimpered before letting out a full-blown howl.

Adam said soothing words to her and held her close to him.

She calmed almost immediately with only a couple of little whimpers.

The crowd started working their way back to Adam and Bree, offering congratulations and good cheer.

Surrounding them first were Adam's family. His brothers—Ray, Cole, Nick and Peter and his sister, Megan.

Megan, her dark hair arranged in a half-up, half-down style, with lots of curls flowing down her back, hugged Bree. "Now, I really have a sister. I've wanted one my whole life and here you are."

Bree loved Megan. She'd known her for years and thought of her as a sister as well. "I'm so glad to have you as a sister, too."

Megan moved to Adam and hugged him, at least, until Lilly pushed her away. "Oh, niece of mine, you are a territorial little thing." Laughing, Megan looked up at Adam. "I guess she wants Daddy all to herself."

He kissed the top of Lilly's head in front of her tiny ponytail. "I don't mind being the most special man in her life at least until she's thirty and then she can start dating."

Bree barked out a laugh. "Thirty, huh? I can't wait to see how that plays out, or in his case, doesn't. You'll be lucky to get her to wait until she's fifteen."

"Then I'll meet every boy and put the fear of God into him if he lays a hand on her."

Bree smiled. She didn't think she'd been this happy in a long time. Not since Brad, but she wouldn't think of their relationship today. This was the first day of the rest of her life. Adam might not think it was forever, but she knew better. She might not have wanted to marry, but she didn't believe in divorce. Their marriage was forever...for better or for worse.

CHAPTER 4

The attendees ate barbeque, swam, and danced to a live band.

Bree enjoyed herself immensely. The first dance was just for Bree and Adam, but she held Lilly while they swayed to Color My World by Chicago. It was one of Bree's favorite songs.

The baby babbled and patted Bree on the cheeks. She grabbed a fistful of Bree's hair.

Adam had to get her to release the locks.

All the women in attendance wanted to hold Lilly, and she was passed around for a while before deciding she'd had enough. She let out a wail.

Bree's new mother-in-law, Madelyn Kincaid, came to her rescue. She took Lilly inside, changed her diaper and was trying to prepare a bottle one-handed.

Bree walked inside. "Here, let me do that." Bree took the bottle and placed water and formula in the bottle before covering the hole in the nipple with one finger and shaking the bottle well to mix it. Then she handed it back to Madelyn, who gave it to Lilly.

The baby was content to have the food and held the bottle herself while her grandmother sat on the sofa in the family room and held her.

"I'm glad you're part of the family, Bree. I didn't know that you and Adam were dating."

Bree saw no reason to lie. "We weren't. This was the best way to have a family for Lilly. I agreed to it because I want to be a mother, and she needed me. I think I fell in love with her the first time I held her in my arms. I knew then that I would do whatever was needed for her, and that meant marrying Adam. We're best friends, so it made sense for him to ask me. I agreed it was the best option for all of us."

But was it, or was it just the best option for her?

* * *

DURING THE RECEPTION, Bree and Adam took turns checking on Lilly after putting her to bed in the playpen in his office at about seven-thirty. Neither of them wanted her as far away from them as she would have been in her crib.

At about ten, it was Bree's turn to check on her and she found the baby awake but not upset.

"Well, hello, my little sweetheart. How are you?" Bree picked her up from the playpen, and as she expected, the baby was soaked. "How about we put you in a dry diaper and some clothes and then give you your bottle? Hmm, how does that sound?"

Lilly babbled.

Bree laughed. She put her on the changing table they bought for Adam's office for when they had Lilly on the first floor. It kept them from having to go upstairs every time she needed changed. She grabbed a clean onesie, diaper, and baby wipes from the drawers under the table.

She was just finishing when Adam came in.

"Ah, I see our daughter has awakened."

"And not a single fuss out of her," replied Bree. "She really is the perfect baby. I know that we have teething and other things to come, and she'll be out of sorts when she's sick, but right now, she's perfect."

He stood next to Bree and ran an index finger down Lilly's cheek. "Maybe that's so we'll fall in love with her."

Bree shrugged, lifted Lilly into her arms. "I don't know why it is. I fell in love with her the first minute I saw her." She turned her gaze toward Adam. "What about you? How long did it really take?"

Adam held his arms out to the baby.

Lilly leaned toward him.

"That's Daddy's little sunshine." He took her into his arms and cuddled her. "The first time she was in my arms, I was a goner. I didn't want to admit that such a little bit of a thing could have that much of a hold over me, but she does. I will move heaven and earth to keep her safe."

Bree thought about it for a moment. "She really is ours, isn't she? Will her mother come back and try to take her?"

Adam frowned. "I'm having my attorney draft a document that will keep Sally from having any rights to Lilly." He reached out with his right arm and wrapped it around Bree's shoulders. "I'll make sure that Lilly is safe from Sally's whims. I don't believe she'll want her back, but she won't be able to do anything if she should change her mind."

Bree leaned into his strong body, feeling his side muscles. She let his words sink in and warm her heart. "Thank you. I didn't want to say anything, afraid I was overstepping my bounds, but—"

"Lilly is as much your daughter as mine now. I don't want you to keep anything from me. We'll make decisions together. If you're worried about something let me know, and we'll figure it out…together."

"Thank you." She wrapped her arms around his waist.

"We're a team. Team Lilly. Don't ever forget that."

"I won't." She moved out from under his arm and looked up at him. "Shall we take our daughter outside? She can say her goodnights to her grandmothers, and they can love on her once more."

"That sounds like a good idea. Then I think I'll leave Ray in charge. My brother can handle anything that comes up. Then the three of us can go to bed. If we're not careful we'll turn her into a night owl."

"You're right. We can't have that. She needs to keep

to her routine. But that doesn't mean we should abandon our guests either. When she's tired, we'll put her back in the playpen."

"You're right." He turned toward the door. "Let's get this done." He walked out toward the crowd in the backyard.

* * *

LILLY WAS in back in her playpen before nine o'clock. She didn't even make a fuss about going down.

Bree and Adam went back to the reception until close to midnight, when they said their goodnights and showed their guests out.

When she got back to her bedroom, Bree took down her hair and brushed it out before braiding it. If she didn't, it would be a rat's nest in the morning, and she hated that. After she was finished, she pulled on her nightgown. The summer garment had spaghetti straps and hit her mid-thigh.

She thought about the commitment they'd just made, not only to Lilly but to each other. Would they eventually fall in love? Could they have a real marriage? Bree was the one who'd put the limit on it. That it just remain that they were friends. She was afraid Adam would never fall in love with her, and she didn't want a marriage just based on sex. Bree needed to be loved. Adam knew this and had never given any indication that he felt more than friendship for her. She wondered if she would be able to only have friendship for their whole marriage. Knowing she needed to be loved didn't bode well for her. If she was to be brutally honest with herself, she'd married Adam as much for him as Lilly. She'd fallen in love with him years ago. She'd thought it was only because she missed Brad, but after much reflection, she knew it wasn't true. Bree loved Adam for himself and for no other reason.

Just as she was about to crawl into bed, a knock sounded on the door.

"Bree? It's Adam."

She grabbed the robe that matched the nightgown and pulled it on before answering the door. "Is it Lilly? I didn't hear anything. I think I need to sleep with the door open."

"It's not Lilly. Now that everyone is gone, I just wondered if you wanted to have a nightcap. Even though it's past midnight, I find I'm not sleepy."

"Um…sure. Why not? For some reason I *am* a little wound up." She walked back to the bed and slid into her slippers. "Shall we?" She noticed Adam was wearing an old t-shirt and sweatpants. "I feel like I'm underdressed for this excursion."

He chuckled. "You're not. I had to put on clothes, so you didn't think I was a pervert or something. I rarely wear anything to bed, but I've decided that with Lilly here, I need to be prepared to be up at a moment's notice and not have to worry about getting dressed whenever she needs me." His gaze roamed over her from head to toe. "We haven't seen each other before bed yet, so I didn't know what you wore to sleep."

"I always wear a nightgown or, in winter, pajamas. I don't like to be cold."

"We can turn the heat up if you like."

"No, that would make everyone else uncomfortable. I can add layers. It's what I did at home because I didn't like the environmental impact of using so much gas, so I'm used to it."

"You do realize we can afford whatever the heating bill is, right?"

She snorted. "Just because we can afford it, doesn't mean we can't still do our bit for conservation."

Adam shrugged. "I suppose that's right. I simply didn't want you to be cold."

Bree reached out and touched his arm. "Thank you, but I'm fine and if I get to the point I'm not, you'll be the first person I come to."

He covered her hand where it rested on his right arm. "Good. I don't want you uncomfortable." He walked down to the recreation room where the bar was located.

The room was set up for watching movies, with six reclining chairs, a couple of loveseat recliners, and a full bar. The TV screen was the largest she'd ever seen. She figured Adam had it custom made. He wasn't one to use anything but the best for his guests.

"What would you like?" Adam slid behind the bar.

Bree sat on one stool. "I would like a chocolate martini."

Adam frowned. "That's the one thing I can't make you. I don't have any Godiva liqueur. If you're feeling like a dessert drink, how about a mudslide?"

"That is my second favorite drink, so bring it on." She leaned her elbows on the teak bar and watched him work. "Ah, you make it with real ice cream. That's the best kind."

"I agree, though in places like Mexico, it's hard to keep ice cream at the beach bar…or the pool bar."

"Don't I know it, but it was still a good drink. At least I didn't have any problems getting completely drunk on them. Do you own a home in Mexico?"

Adam set the drink, which he'd put in an over-sized martini glass, in front of her. "I do. I have several homes all over the world. I happen to use the one in Mexico the most. It's right on the beach in Cancun."

"That sounds wonderful. What are you having to drink? Something special for our wedding night?"

"I'm having my old standby of a Manhattan."

"You are a man of habit. Though, I think you'll have to be making new habits with Lilly here."

He came around the bar and sat on the stool next to Bree. "And I'm more than willing to make them. Working from home for a while is just the first. I plan on making a place for her in my office, so I can take her to work when I need to…or want to."

"I'll be with her during the day. You don't have to worry about that."

"I know I don't, but I want to be able to take her

with me. I want to show off my daughter to my employees."

Bree laughed. "That makes perfect sense, especially since most of those employees never thought you'd marry or have children. You're thirty-six now. You're getting long in the tooth, as my mother would say."

He snorted. "And what about you, dear wife? Are you on the shelf, as *my* mother would say? You're twenty-eight now. That used to mean you were an old maid…destined to be a spinster and live alone except for your hundreds of cats."

She lifted a brow. "Ha ha. Very funny. Well, no one is an old maid or long in the tooth anymore. We stopped those rumors today."

He frowned. "And started an entirely new set of rumors."

Bree took a sip of her drink. The creamy, chocolatey mixture sliding down as easily and any ice cream shake. "This is great. Thank you." She took another sip and smiled.

"You're easy to please." He chuckled before he took a cocktail napkin and wiped away the mustache, she'd given herself.

"Thanks." She took the napkin and wiped her mouth again.

"You're welcome."

They talked and drank their cocktails.

Before she knew it, she'd had three of the drinks and was feeling a pleasant buzz.

"Adam."

"Hmm?"

"I want to kiss you."

His eyebrows practically leaped off his forehead as they went so high, so fast. Then his expression settled, and he cocked up one side of his mouth. "That's good, because I want to kiss you, too." He slipped an arm around her waist and leaned over, pulling her close at the same time.

"You do?" She went willingly.

"I definitely do. Very much," he whispered when he was a hair's breadth away.

The moment his lips touched hers, Bree was lost. She let herself go, enjoying the way warmth spread through her body and the feel of his soft, yet firm lips.

After a few moments, he pulled back, resting his forehead against hers. "That was nice. I want you, Bree. More than I've ever wanted anyone."

"I want you, too. But we can't. You know that and I know that. We're best friends and I don't want to risk that."

Adam slowly shook his head. "We are best friends, we're also husband and wife. We can do this. Let me make love to you?"

Should she? Was she wrong to expect their marriage to be forever and never make love, never have more children. Was she wrong to just want their friendship? Could she ask that of Adam? But she needed to be loved...utterly and completely, like she and Brad had loved each other. What would Brad say about what she'd done? She was so tempted...and very scared. She knew having sex would complicate things and if something happened, it might break them apart irrevocably.

"I can't, Adam. You know that. In your heart of hearts, you know that."

Adam sighed. "I do know that, and I don't want to risk our friendship either. I know that you still mourn Brad. In some ways I do, too. Although right now I wish he would just go away and not come between us."

"Adam—" Her heart was breaking. She was fouling Adam's memory of Brad and that is not what she wanted

He raised a hand and shook his head. "No, I'm being honest. I won't apologize for wanting you, wanting the marriage to be real, but I know that is impossible at this point in time."

She bobbed her head. "It is." *For now. Perhaps sometime in the future, but I'm not ready. I know that. I need love, and not just the physical, but the emotional, too.*

wo months later

BREE AND ADAM sat having their morning coffee at the large round table in the kitchen's nook. "Bree, we are attending a get-together at the home of the man whose company I want to acquire, a week from today. If you need a dress, you'd better hurry and pick it out. It's a formal affair. He wants everyone in tuxes and evening gowns."

"That seems odd for a "get-together", she made finger quotes. "That term makes it sound like it would be a casual outing."

Adam shrugged. "I know but it is what it is."

"Well, it so happens, I've been looking at this gorgeous gown online, and I've seen it at a boutique at the Cherry Creek shopping center. I'll head down there today with Lilly. I'm sure the ladies there will love to watch Lilly while I try the dress on, assuming they have my size."

"And if they don't?"

"They have lots of gowns, so I'll find something appropriate. Don't worry."

"Get Lilly a fancy little outfit while you're out. I'm sure she'll look adorable."

"Oh, face it, you'll like whatever she's dressed in because she is adorable. Have you asked Carole to babysit?"

"No, I thought we'd take her to my parents for the night. Mom will love having her granddaughter overnight. Then we can go to breakfast and pick her up the following day. They probably would have come and picked her up, but I don't want them driving at night. It's too dangerous."

"I agree. That sounds good. Madelyn will be thrilled."

"My thoughts exactly."

"The boutique opens at ten. I'll be there right when they open and still be home in time to put Lilly down for her nap, even though she'll probably fall asleep in the car on the way home."

Bree stood.

Adam did, too. He took Bree in his arms.

She smiled and looked up at him. "What's this about?"

"I just wanted to hug you." Then he leaned down,

kissed her forehead, and then her cheek. "Have fun today."

She pulled back, her forehead wrinkled and cocked her head a little, then she gave it a slow shake. "Oh, I will. I like nothing better than spending your money." *I wonder what he meant by those kisses. That's not like him.*

He barked out a laugh. "If only that were true. You never buy anything for yourself. Now, Lilly, that's a different story. Neither of us can resist buying her things. We'll have to start using one of the other bedrooms for all her toys."

Laughing, Bree stepped back out of his arms. "On that note, you need to go to work, and I need to get showered while Lilly is having her morning nap."

He released her. "Okay, I'm outta here. See you tonight. I want a fashion show after dinner. You and Lilly."

"I think that can be arranged. By the way, who is this person having the get-together?"

"People. Wade and Stacy Danvers, from Danvers Industries. They are the same couple we had to get married for in order to even be in the running for acquiring his company."

"Ah. I understand. I should get something conservative today then."

"Not on your life. I want to show off my beautiful wife. Get something sexy that shows off your figure."

"In that case, the dress I have in mind is perfect. I could show you online, but I think you'll enjoy the surprise more if I wear it."

"That's fine, I'll see it when I get home. Have a great day." He left through the door to the garage.

Bree wondered if it was such a good idea to have Lilly staying with Madelyn and Rocky overnight. She and Adam had been dancing around each other since the night of the wedding. They hadn't indulged in anymore late-night kisses, but could they in a week, when Lilly was gone? Was she playing with fire if they did?

ONE WEEK LATER

BREE HADN'T GIVEN Adam a fashion show when she bought the dress so this would be the first time he had seen it. She walked down the stairs to the large foyer at the front door. Her dress rustled just the slightest as she moved.

Adam was there, with Lilly, waiting. "About time, we're—" He looked up and nothing came out of his mouth. Then he recovered and whistled. "Wow. You look spectacular."

She was pleased with his reaction. After seeing herself in the full-length mirror in her room, when she'd finished getting ready, she had to agree. She looked amazing in this dress.

The dress was a dark midnight-blue and covered in thousands of tiny crystal beads, so the garment looked like she was wearing the night sky. It literally shimmered when she moved, catching every ray of light in the room. She wore sandals with a tiny black strap over her toes and one around her ankle. They had four-inch heels and forced her to take small steps or risk spraining an ankle or, worse yet, breaking a leg.

The bodice of the dress had spaghetti straps, a deep V-neckline, and skimmed her body to below the hips where it flared out to the hem, allowing lots of movement with every step. She held a small evening clutch covered in the same material as the dress, crystals and all.

She turned in a circle, and the skirt of the garment swung out, baring her legs as it did. When she halted, the dress shimmered to a stop. She gazed at Adam. "Well, what do you think? Will I do, or is it too much for the *get-together* tonight?"

Adam closed his mouth. "You look beautiful. I love the gown. I think it's perfect for tonight. Do you need a wrap? The air gets a little chilly after the sun goes down."

"I have a matching shawl. The weather is still warm enough the shawl should be enough." She looked at him up and down. "You look very handsome in your tux. I haven't seen you in one for years. I'd forgotten how well you filled one out."

Adam looked down at Lilly. "Don't you think your mommy looks beautiful? Hmm. Pretty, huh?"

She looked over at Bree and held her arms out. "Mama. Mama."

With tears in her eyes, Bree took the baby from Adam. "Did you hear her? She said 'mama'. Her first word. Oh, I think I'm going to cry."

Adam placed his hand on her shoulder and squeezed. "Don't do that, honey. You'll ruin your makeup."

She flashed him a gaze that she hoped said she didn't think he was funny. "I'll cry if I want to and if it ruins my makeup, I'll fix it."

Adam backed up a step, his hands up in front of him. "Sorry. You're right, but I don't like to see you cry. It…hurts me."

Bree got a lump in her throat when she looked at him. "Ah, I don't want to hurt you. I'm just happy. They would be happy tears."

He frowned and his eyebrows furrowed. "They are still tears. I don't like it."

She grinned. "Okay. How about you take our girl here and get her in her car seat and I'll get the diaper bag?"

Adam took Lilly from Bree. "Come on, sweet pea. You get to spend the night with Grandma. She and Grandpa will spoil you rotten and you'll have a great time. Mom bought a bed for her. Did I tell you that?"

Shaking her head, Bree grabbed the diaper bag off the living room sofa. "No, but I'm not surprised. She wanted to be prepared. I would have done the same."

He walked out to the garage and settled Lilly into the back of the Lincoln Navigator.

Adam bought the vehicle specifically because it was safer for Lilly.

Bree placed the bag in the backseat next to Lilly. She pulled out a teething ring for her to play with and chew on during the trip to Adam's parents' ranch. The journey would take them close to an hour because the ranch was about forty miles away. Then they would have to double back to Denver and the party at the Danver's home.

Adam said the couple was old-fashioned.

Bree thought about the circumstances of her marriage and didn't regret her decision for one moment. She was happy. The only problem was she was falling in love with Adam, and she was fairly sure he was falling in love with her.

He wasn't at the point of admitting it to her, but she felt it just the same.

They arrived at Madelyn and Rocky's home pulling into the driveway.

Madelyn rushed out of the front door and was down the steps and next to the SUV practically before Adam cut the engine.

At just over five feet tall, with a slender frame, the woman wasn't very big. Her still blonde hair was shot through with gray and pulled into a long braid down her back.

"Where is my baby?" the older woman said as she opened the back door and extricated Lilly from her car seat. "There is my girl." She pulled the baby into her arms and hugged her, then placed little kisses all over Lilly's face.

Lilly giggled at her grandmother's antics.

"Come on inside. You have a few minutes, don't you?"

"Yes, we can come in for just a minute." Adam came around the vehicle and helped Bree to the ground.

Madelyn turned her gaze toward Bree. "You look beautiful, my dear."

"Thank you. I want us to make a good impression on his future client."

Adam grinned and placed a hand at her waist as they headed inside. "She sounds so sure this guy will be my client. I like a wife with a positive outlook."

"You should," intoned a gravelly voice. Adam's father, Rocky, stood just inside the screened-in porch. It faced west so they could see the mountains. He and Madelyn came out here and had coffee in the spring, summer and fall months. He held the door open for Madelyn and Lilly. And then for Bree.

In looking at Rocky, Bree saw what Adam would look like in thirty years. Tall and fit, with wide streaks of silver shooting through his dark hair on each side of his head at the temples. Those same blue-gray eyes twinkled with mischief. And at the outer corner of his eyes were wrinkles from a lifetime of sorrows and laughter.

Adam held the door, while his father followed the women in.

Rocky began tickling Lilly, making her giggle. And

he talked baby talk to her, eliciting laughter from the rest of the adults.

"What?" He lifted his shoulders and put out his hands, palms up. "She understands me, don't you buttercup?"

Adam shook his head, but he was smiling. "We need to get going. I don't want to be late to this function."

"No. Definitely not." She turned her gaze toward Madelyn. "Call if you need us."

Madelyn rolled her eyes. "We'll be fine. I raised six rambunctious children. I think I can handle one sweet baby."

"And I'll help, too." Rocky kept his attention on Lilly. "Son, I know you and Bree are nervous leaving her for the first time, but everything will be okay. Your mom and I are good at this. You'll see. Now, go. Have a good time at your party tonight, and we'll see you tomorrow for brunch."

Adam chuckled. "Okay, we're going."

Bree leaned over and gave Lilly a kiss. "You be good for Grandma and Grandpa. Can you do that for Mama?"

"Mama. Mama."

Bree still wanted to cry from happiness.

"Oh, when did our girl start talking?" Madelyn smiled at Lilly.

"Tonight, as we were about to leave. I almost cried," said Bree.

"But I made her angry, and then she didn't want to cry anymore," said Adam.

Bree widened her eyes. "Are you saying you did that on purpose?"

Adam shrugged. "It worked, didn't it? Does it really matter if I did it on purpose or not, as long as the desired outcome was achieved."

"Oh, men!" cursed Bree.

Adam laughed. "Let's go. You can be mad at me in the car on the way to the party."

"Oh, don't worry, I will be."

The drive to the party was quiet for the first half as Bree stewed.

"I can't believe you manipulated me like that." She crossed her arms over her chest.

"I didn't plan it. It just happened."

"Well, don't let it happen again. I don't like it."

"Oh, Bree. You know I didn't do it on purpose…at least, consciously. I definitely didn't want to be late, though, and that might have played into it."

She rolled her eyes and leaned her head back against the headrest, knowing since her hair was done in curls down to the middle of her back, it wouldn't be messed up. "Okay. It didn't hurt anything, but you should know, if anyone asks about Lilly, that's what I'm leading with. Her first word." Bree couldn't help but smile. "Mama. I still can't believe it."

Adam chuckled. "We've both been working with her to say it. I don't know why you're surprised."

"Because she said it without coaxing, and she knew that it meant me. She held out her arms." She patted her chest.

He reached over and laid his right hand on her leg. "I'm glad you're so happy. You deserve every bit of happiness, Bree. I want you to know that."

She covered his hand with hers. "I am happy, Adam. I didn't know I would ever be this happy again after losing Brad. But it's like he's here and telling me it's time to let go. Time to grab for my happiness."

Adam stared at her.

It was still light outside, and she could see his face. "Adam? What is it?"

He closed his eyes, swallowed and shook his head. "It's just odd, because I've been feeling the same thing. I mean literally. It's like Brad has been here for me, too. Saying it's time to move on. To let the past go and embrace the future."

"I agree with him. We need to concentrate on Lilly. She is my happiness."

"I know and I'm glad. She's definitely mine, too."

Bree wondered if Adam could truly be happy in a marriage like theirs. He was a man, after all, and had never been a celibate one. He and Brad used to laugh over his conquests. Was it just because Adam had never found love? Would he even be open to it if he saw it? Could he eventually love her?

CHAPTER 6

They arrived at the party. The building was huge with two stories and huge double doors. It was the biggest house she'd ever seen. It had to be at least thirty thousand square feet.

Adam hurried around to help her from the SUV. Then he handed his keys to the valet.

Bree leaned toward Adam and whispered, "I've never seen a valet at a private residence before."

They stood and looked up at the building.

Adam placed his hand at Bree's waist as they walked up the stairs. "This isn't his residence. This is the country club. I thought it would be at his home, but I didn't pay much attention to the address. Obviously, I was mistaken."

"Actually, that's good. I won't feel like I'm being nosy when I have a look around."

They entered through the open double doors into a foyer with another set of double doors directly in front of them. The foyer went the length of the building and was about fifteen feet wide.

Adam opened the right side of the interior double doors and then held out his arm to her.

She placed her hand in the crook of his elbow. They stopped first at the coatroom where Bree gave over her wrap. She put the ticket into her clutch and took Adam's arm again.

He led them inside, where he released her arm and grabbed them each a glass of champagne from the tray held by a server.

Bree took hers with her left hand and sipped the drink while looking around her. The room was painted a cream color with dark wood trim. The bar was old-looking, made from a dark wood, maybe mahogany, and was about fifteen or twenty feet long. Large windows were across both of the walls on the east and west sides of the room. The area was open and was full, but yet not overly crowded. Tables were set up along the windows, leaving the center open and easily navigable.

She stuck close to Adam. He knew these people she didn't.

"Well, well. Look who the cat dragged in," said a man with graying brown hair.

"Simon," said Adam.

Bree could feel distaste when Adam said his name.

"Aren't you going to introduce me to your lovely companion?"

Adam took a deep breath. "Simon Chandler, this is my wife, Brianna Kincaid."

Bree extended her right hand. "Mr. Chandler."

Simon took her hand and brought it to his lips, kissing the top. "Mrs. Kincaid. I'd heard that Adam married, I hadn't realized you were so beautiful. He's a lucky man."

Bree pulled her hand back. "Thank you."

Adam looked around and behind Simon. "Where is your better half tonight, Simon. Janie is the only reason most people put up with you."

Simon's lip curled up. "She was feeling poorly. I brought someone else." He looked over Adam's shoulder. "Ah, here she comes now."

Bree turned at the same time Adam did.

"Valerie." She nodded her head curtly.

"Brianna. I'd heard you and Adam married. I couldn't believe it and only three years after poor Brad's death."

Bree narrowed her eyes, wishing her gaze was lasers that could zap the other woman out of existence. "I hadn't heard you were dating again after the last fiasco."

Valerie, a tall, bleached blonde, wore a red dress with a slit to the top of her left thigh. The dress was sleeveless, with a deep V-neck almost to her belly button, and she wore long, red lace gloves.

Bree thought she looked like a vampire wannabe.

Valerie looked Bree up and down, before turning

toward Adam. "Yes, well we all make mistakes. Mine was obviously letting Adam go."

Adam narrowed his eyes. "You didn't let me go, Valerie. I kicked you out when I found you'd cheated on me. As the saying goes, you made your bed and then you had to lie in it. I wasn't about to let you stick around."

Valerie shrugged. "Yes, I admit that wasn't my finest hour."

Adam placed a hand on Bree's back and started massaging the tension out of her muscles.

He frowned, but didn't remove his hand from Bree's back. "You're just sorry you got caught, not that you did it in the first place."

She waved a hand in front of her. "Of course, I am. I screwed myself and thought I could get away with the affair with Simon. I found you a little too vanilla for my tastes. It doesn't matter now, I'm here and that's all I want at the moment."

"You haven't changed since college. The one I feel sorry for in this mess."—Bree looked directly at Simon with disgust— "is your wife. Janie. You remember her. Nice woman unlucky enough to be married to you."

"She's fine." Simon sneered. "She's getting exactly what she wanted—access to my money—It keeps her happy, and I can still have Valerie when I want her. Like tonight. She looks much better on my arm than Janie."

A man with gray hair and mustache approached unseen by either Simon, Adam, or Valerie.

But Bree saw him.

He didn't look happy.

The man frowned. "Mr. Chandler. I had hoped you would bring your wife."

Simon reddened. "Ah, Mr. Danvers…my wife was indisposed so I opted to bring Ms. Valerie Kincaid rather than come alone."

"Kincaid?" He cocked an eyebrow and looked at Adam. "Your ex-wife I assume."

"Yes, Mr. Danvers." Adam put his arm around Bree's shoulders. "Brianna is my wife and the mother of our child. Brianna, may I present Mr. Wade Danvers?"

"I'm pleased to meet you Mr. Danvers," Bree extended her right hand.

Danvers shook it. "It's nice to meet you, too, Brianna. May I call you Brianna?"

"Of course, but my friends call me Bree and I think we will be good friends."

Wade crooked his arm. "Would you be so kind as to accompany me to meet my dear wife. I'm afraid she doesn't get around like she used to. Arthritis in her knees has her confined to a wheelchair for these gatherings."

Bree took his arm, then looked back at Adam and lifted her shoulders just a bit.

"Don't worry, my dear, Bree. Adam will be right behind us." Danvers turned and looked at Adam. "Follow us, would you dear boy?"

"Of course." Adam shot Simon a triumphant grin.

When they arrived, the small, silver-haired woman

in the wheelchair smiled broadly. She was lovely. Her hair was in a sleek chignon, and she wore a stylish black evening gown.

Wade released Bree's arm, walked to his wife, and kissed her on the forehead. "How are you, my love?"

She patted his hand. "I'm fine, Wade." Then she turned toward Bree and Adam. "You don't have to worry about me. Introduce me to this lovely couple you've brought to see me."

"Adam and Bree Kincaid, this is my wife, Stacy."

Bree moved next to the woman and held out her right hand. "I'm very pleased to meet you."

"And I you." Stacy looked Bree up and down. "You are just the prettiest little thing. I love that dress. It looks like something I would have worn when I could still walk."

"Thank you. I love it, too." She ran a hand over her stomach. She loved the material. Even with all the crystals, the dress still felt wonderful. "When Adam said we were coming and to buy a new dress, I was thrilled. But listen to me. I'm just rambling."

She extended her hand toward Adam. "I'm pleased to meet you, Mr. Kincaid."

Adam smiled and turned his attention to Stacy. He took her hand and kissed the top. "Call me Adam, please."

"Adam." Stacy nodded. "Wade has told me a lot about you. He's very enamored with you." She chuckled. "I don't mean that the way it sounds. He likes your business practices and that you've married. I understand you have a baby daughter?"

Bree grinned, her heartwarming with the thought of her baby daughter. "Oh, we do, and she said her first word today. Mama, while she reached for me, so she knows what is means, too."

"That's wonderful." Stacy smiled. "I remember when our kids were that age. How old is your daughter, by the way?"

Bree couldn't stop herself from the pride she felt being Lilly's mother. "Lilly just turned eight months. She's also turtle-crawling on the floor. We have to watch her like a hawk. I caught her half-way under the bed the other day."

They all laughed.

"We did the same thing with our oldest. Being new parents is hard, but it gets easier with the next ones," said Wade.

Adam and Bree looked at each other, agreeing in silence not to comment.

Bree would like nothing more than to have more children with Adam. She knew she was in love with him. She still missed Brad, but Adam had taken care of her. Made sure she got everything Brad had wanted her to get. Brad had left her a wealthy woman in her own right. She didn't need or want Adam's money. That was probably appealing to Adam, since his ex, Valerie, had been all about the money.

But Valerie had signed a prenup and got very little. Bree thought maybe he was feeling a little guilty over

Valerie's having had an affair. She knew he thought if he'd been home more often, it might not have happened. That was why he'd been generous with Valerie, giving her the condo they lived in and the car she drove.

Bree knew differently. She'd known the woman was cheating even before Valerie and Adam had married. Bree had tried telling Adam, but he was in love, or so he said, and didn't listen to her, and Valerie had hurt him.

She turned her attention back to Stacy and Wade. "So, Wade, what does Danvers Industries actually do?"

Wade placed one hand behind his back and the other on Stacy's shoulder. "We're like Kincaid Holdings. We have a portfolio of companies we own and manage. It's much easier having them all under one roof so to speak instead of having fifteen different companies."

Bree was interested in what Adam did, but he wasn't very forthcoming about it, so now that she had a captive audience, she meant to take advantage of it. "Are the companies all in one sector of industry?"

Wade chuckled. "It would make it a lot easier if they were, but they are different for the sake of diversity. If one industry goes down, we have others that will offset it and often pick up the slack left by the other companies. You're passionately interested in business, aren't you?"

She nodded. "I am. I hope to open my own business one day, but I want to be there for Lilly before I decide on anything else. I'm an author now which will allow me to care for Lilly, but I want to have something else to fall back on. Something physical. Perhaps when she starts school, I'll have more time to think about it."

"And what business would you like to open?" asked Stacy.

Bree realigned her body, so she faced Stacy directly and then gazed down at her. "I love to garden, so that's what I'd like to do…have a garden center. It would carry everything you could want for a lovely backyard garden."

"It sounds like you've given this some thought. Have you done anymore planning?" asked Wade.

Bree shook her head. "Right now, it's just a dream. Like I said I don't want to start anything until Lilly is older. She's the most important person in my life."

"I understand she's a baby and needs you, but you can't live your life just for your children. That's unfair to you and to them. Trust me on this. I did that with my first one, and he resented me for not letting him grow up like his classmates." Stacy chuckled at the memory. "We learned and treated the rest of the children differently."

"I'll take your advice under advisement." Bree wasn't sure she could do what they suggested, but she'd at least think about it. As the oldest in a family of five kids, she'd always been the one responsible for her younger siblings. Her parents were always working. Bree wanted to be there for Lilly in a way her parents never were.

The two couples chatted for a good thirty minutes.

"If you could direct me to the powder room, I'd appreciate it," Bree whispered to Stacy.

Stacy pointed toward the entrance doors. "Of course. It's just off the lobby where you came in. You can't miss the signs."

"Thank you." Bree turned her gaze to Adam. "I'll be right back."

"Certainly. We'll be here." Adam gave her a kiss on the forehead.

Bree lifted her eyebrows. She had her back to Wade and Stacy, so only Adam could see her reaction.

He simply smiled.

Then she remembered what they were trying to convey and relaxed. Tonight, they were a happily married couple with a baby at home…well, at Rocky and Madelyn's.

"Excuse me. I'll be right back." She headed off in the direction Stacy had indicated.

She was fixing her lipstick in the reclining room mirror when Valerie Kincaid walked up next to her. Bree looked at the woman in the mirror. "Valerie."

Valerie narrowed her eyes and looked down her nose at Bree. "Brianna. I was surprised to hear of your marriage to Adam. I suppose I should say congratulations."

Bree lifted a brow and placed the lipstick into her evening bag. "Don't bother on my account."

Valerie laughed. "You're a little snippy tonight,

aren't you? Marriage to Adam not all you thought it would be?"

"My marriage to Adam is wonderful and not any of your business, anyway." Would her expression give her away? She smiled, though it didn't reach her eyes. Valerie wouldn't see that, though. The woman was too vapid to notice anything.

Valerie's smile disappeared. "My marriage to Adam wasn't anyone's business, either, but Brad didn't seem to have any problems sticking his nose into it. I know it was him who told Adam about me."

Bree wouldn't have Brad's memory savaged. "You're wrong about that, but even if you were right about Brad, you were wrong to cheat on Adam. All he ever did was love you, but that wasn't enough for you, was it? And with Simon? What in the world were you thinking? Simon will never divorce Janie. She owns more than fifty-two percent of the business. He'd be a fool to divorce her."

"You take that back. You're wrong about that." Valerie hissed.

Bree laughed. Adam had briefed her about Simon and explained Janie's part of the business. He knew he'd have to work with Janie more than Simon. "You should do your homework better before you decide to seduce someone else's husband. Janie's parents started the business. She was gifted it upon her marriage to Simon. He was the means to an end. She wanted the business, and her parents wouldn't give it to her until she was married. As part of her dowry, for lack of a better word, Simon was given his part of the business when he married Janie. Theirs is a business arrangement more than a marriage."

Valerie eyes narrowed and her lips lifted on one side.

Bree thought steam might spray from her ears at any moment. The look on Valerie's face was priceless, and Bree had to smile, though when she thought of her own marriage of convenience, her smile faltered. She and Adam had the same kind of arrangement. A business arrangement. Her smile disappeared.

Valerie narrowed her eyes and slapped Bree across the face.

Bree's hand immediately went to her left cheek. It stung and she was afraid there would be a hand print. "What was that for?"

"Because you're lying. You're trying to make me angry, and you achieved your goal."

Bree stiffened and her eyes narrowed. "I'm not lying and if you lay a hand on me again, you'll be sorry. If you don't believe me, ask Simon. See what he tells you. Or better yet, ask Janie. Do you think your little affair will be news to her? I guarantee she's known about it since it happened."

For the first time, Valerie's eyes widened and she stepped back.

Bree saw it in the other woman's face as her confidence wavered.

She wasn't prepared to let go of her plans, maybe even dreams, that Simon would leave Janie for her.

Bree laughed. "You realize I'm right, and you don't know what to do. You've hitched your wagon to Simon only to find the tires are flat. Good luck, with that and leave me alone." She headed to the door.

"You know he'll never love you."

Bree turned back and faced Valerie. "What?"

"Adam. He'll never love you. He's not capable."

"Maybe you were just the wrong woman and maybe that's not what I'm looking for." She didn't believe her. Bree was sure that Adam had loved Valerie, but what if she was right and Bree was wrong?

Valerie laughed, the sound anything but humorous. "Oh, you're looking for it. I see it in your eyes when you gaze at him. You're already in love with him, or well on your way there. Don't let him fool you. Adam Kincaid is only out for Adam Kincaid."

"You're entitled to your opinion, but I'll tell you now, you're wrong. I'm getting exactly what I need from Adam." With those words, Bree opened the door and headed out to rejoin the others.

Was Valerie right? Would Adam never be able to love her? She was correct about one thing…Bree was in love with Adam. Now to figure out what to do about it.

CHAPTER 7

Bree rejoined Adam and the Danvers with a smile she knew didn't quite reach her eyes.

Adam gazed over at her, his smile faltering as he lifted a brow, but didn't say anything.

About that time, an old song began to play,. "Color My World" by Chicago.

Adam put out his arm to Bree. "Would you do me the honor of dancing with me?"

"Oh…I." She looked at Stacy and Wade. She wasn't sure she should be that close to Adam and hoped the Danvers would save her.

"Go on, my dear," said Stacy. "This is one of my favorite songs and if I could, I'd be out there dancing alongside of you."

Bree smiled at the woman and then turned to Adam. "I'd love to." She placed her hand in the crook of his left elbow.

He covered her hand with his right, and they made

their way to the dance floor on the west side of the room.

Adam wrapped his arms around Bree's waist and pulled her close.

Bree wrapped her arms around his neck and rested her head on his chest. Being in his arms calmed her.

He leaned down and placed his cheek on the top of her head. "Do you want to tell me what happened in the bathroom? And why your left cheek is red like someone hit you?"

Bree sighed. "I ran into Valerie in the bathroom. I might have told her the truth about Simon and Janie's marriage."

He leaned back to meet her gaze. "The truth?"

"Yes, what you told me. That Janie owns fifty-two percent of Simon's company, that he will never leave her, and that Janie knows about their affair and doesn't care. She didn't take the information well. She slapped me and called me a liar." She felt him stiffen.

"She shouldn't have hit you. You weren't lying about Simon."

They swayed to the music, and, for some reason, Bree felt mostly content. She had a handsome husband who had his arms around her. She liked the feel of his body against hers. Bree fit him in all the right places, like she'd been made just for him. She loved him, and she hoped he would someday love her. And she also had a beautiful daughter who had called her *mama* for the first time that day. Remembering brought tears of joy to her eyes, but she held them back. She didn't want to ruin this moment for anything.

"What are you thinking?"

She turned her gaze up to his. "I was thinking about Lilly." Bree couldn't help but smile. "She makes me so happy and not just because she's a good baby. Even though she's teething, she's not overly cranky which is a feat I'm not used to seeing. My brothers especially were horrible when they were going through it. Every one of them cried and carried on like they were dying."

Adam chuckled. "Maybe they were just big wusses…like they are now."

Bree laughed. "I think I'm supposed to be insulted, except I agree. I think they're growing up though. Even Mother says so."

"How is your mother? We haven't talked about her very much since we got married."

She noticed the other dancers for the first time and realized she'd thought she and Adam were alone in the room. In her cocoon, she saw and heard only him. "Living the dream. Seriously, Mom's doing great and seems happy. Dad is, too. They've become better friends since he retired, which surprises me. Did you know that she and Janie Chandler's mother are friends?"

"I did not."

She leaned back and looked Adam in the eyes. He held her close, his arms around her waist. "Do you think Janie will ever divorce Simon? I don't think he's a very smart man other than he married Janie."

Adam chortled. "Janie always was a smart woman. I never understood her marrying Simon, but knowing her, she had a good reason. Whatever it was she needed from him she got and now she's done with him. She leaves him to his dalliances and keeps control of the business."

"My guess is she wanted children, at least one of each and that is exactly what she got. Once she had her children she was done with him. She might divorce him, but I think that's unlikely. She's comfortable and sees no reason to change."

"So, you think she only married him to get her children?"

"I do. I don't think Janie actually likes him at all. Keeping Simon is insurance that no one bothers her, and she can live her life as she wants. She has her own money, makes her own decisions and doesn't have to share, or ask permission or answer to anyone."

Adam swayed to the music. "It's not unlike us. You married me so you could have a child."

She stiffened her back before she realized what she was doing and relaxed again. "And you married me to have a wife and mother to Lilly."

"Do you regret marrying me?"

"No," said Bree, not missing a beat. "As far as I'm concerned, it was the best thing I have ever done. I wouldn't give up Lilly for anything." She lowered her gaze and rested her head against his chest again.

He was a good head taller than she was, so she fit perfectly under his chin.

"Do you regret marrying me?" Bree didn't look up, but kept her head on his chest.

"I don't."

She pulled back and stared into his eyes. "I'm glad."

He pulled her tight against his body. "Good."

They danced for a while longer, then Adam pulled back and took her by the hand. "Let's go home. We've made nice for long enough. We'll say our goodbyes to Wade and Stacy and then leave."

"Sounds good." She didn't pull her hand out of his, but walked by his side over to the Danvers.

"We need to be going." Adam extended a hand to Wade. "This has been a nice evening. Thank you for inviting us."

Wade took Adam's hand and shook it, then looked around at the crowd. "It has been a good get-together. I'll have my assistant get in touch with you so we can talk business."

"Yes, sir, I'd like that."

Bree went to Stacy and held out a hand. "Thank you for everything. I've not enjoyed myself this much in a long time."

Stacy took her hand lightly and squeezed it. "I enjoyed talking to you, my dear. I hope we can do it again soon."

"I hope so, too. I'd love to have you meet my daughter, Lilly. She would absolutely adore you."

"That would be lovely." Stacy's mouth turned down.

Her sadness was clear.

Stacy's eyes were glassy. "My children have all

moved away from Denver, so I don't get to see my grandchildren as often as I would like. I'm afraid traveling is difficult for me, and even though the kids come out several times a year, it's not enough for me to really get to know my grandchildren."

"You are welcome in our home anytime. Call me, and we'll make the arrangements, or we can come to you. Whichever you prefer."

Stacy looked down for a moment and then turned a radiant smile on Bree. "Having you come to me would probably be the easiest."

"Then that's what we'll do. Lilly loves traveling in the car, though she might fall asleep before we get there." Bree shook her head and laughed. "But she wakes up happy, so that isn't a problem."

"Perhaps you could come for tea on Tuesday, say around two?"

Bree nodded. "That sounds good. We'll be there. What's your address?"

Stacy rattled off the address. "Better yet," she reached into her evening bag, came back with a business card, and handed it to Bree. "Then it's a date. This has our address and my private number."

Bree looked at the card and then tucked it into her clutch. "I would never have thought to have a business card with me."

Stacy chuckled. "I learned a long time ago to carry them. You never know when a business opportunity or a personal one, will come up."

"That's really smart. I'll have to get some made."

Adam sidled up next to Bree and placed an arm around her waist. "Are you ready?"

"I am," answered Bree.

He stepped nearer to Stacy, took her right hand, and kissed the top. "Thank you for your delightful hospitality."

Wade stepped close to his wife and rested a hand on her shoulder.

"We've enjoyed having you." Stacy looked at Bree. "I'll see you on Tuesday."

"Definitely." Bree smiled before turning toward Wade. "It was nice meeting you."

The older man smiled. "It was a delight meeting you. I think Adam did very well for himself with you."

Adam lifted a brow. "I have to agree. Goodnight, now."

They walked out to the coatroom and Bree retrieved her wrap. Then they got the SUV from the valet.

The drive home was quiet, but not uncomfortable. Because of the lack of traffic out at that time of night, it only took them about fifteen minutes to get home.

After pulling into the garage, Adam killed the engine and hurried around to help Bree from the vehicle.

He looked down at her shoes and shook his head. "I don't know how you manage to walk in those things. What if you had to run?"

"I'd kick them off and never look back. You didn't

seem to mind when I fit directly under your chin when we danced."

They stepped into the kitchen as Adam chortled. "No, I didn't, did I. I have to admit, I like how we fit together."

Her lips tipped up. "It was nice. I've never danced with anyone who I fit with so well." She walked to the island and laid her clutch and her wrap on the counter.

"Not even Brad?"

Bree's smile slipped. "Not even Brad." *Brad only danced with me a couple of times. He hated dancing, but he did it for me.*

He stepped toward her and clasped her hands in his. "I'm sorry. I shouldn't have brought him up. Let's have a cocktail and talk about something else."

She nodded and pulled back her hands. "We didn't think to eat at the party. Do you want me to whip up something? I think we still have some roast pork from dinner last night. It would make great sandwiches."

He leaned on the island. "That sounds good. White bread, please. I'll get the drinks. What would you like?"

"Something simple and fruity." She placed an index finger on her chin. "How about a pina colada? Do we have the ingredients for that?"

"We do. It's one of Carole's favorite drinks. She always makes sure to keep them stocked." He walked away toward the stairs, heading down to the movie room and the bar, next to it.

While he was gone, Bree got out the roasted pork

leftovers and made them each a sandwich. By the time she finished, she saw Adam returning with the drinks.

"Here you go." He handed her one of the glasses.

He'd even garnished it with a quarter slice of pineapple and a pink umbrella.

"Wow, just like at a real bar." She held up her glass for a toast. "To best friends."

Adam eyed her for a moment and then raised his glass. "To best friends."

I wonder if we can be more to each other. Would I be jeopardizing our friendship if I let him know I wanted more?

After they finished their sandwiches and drinks, they cleaned the kitchen together.

"You know," said Adam. "Carole will do this in the morning. It's kind of what I pay her for."

Bree sighed. She still wasn't used to having a house-keeper. "I don't want to leave her a mess. She has enough to do with keeping the house up as it is."

Adam shrugged. "Your wish is my command." He waggled his brows.

Bree laughed, as she was sure he intended.

After they were done in the kitchen, they made their way to the movie room. They sat on a sofa, watched *The Avengers: Endgame* and she had a couple more pina coladas.

Bree curled up next to Adam and leaned against his side.

He put his arm around her shoulders, anchoring her.

They were almost like a real married couple.

She wondered if they would ever have a genuine marriage. One where they loved each other and had more children. She had to admit, she longed for that. She and Adam had been married for over two months but had been best friends for much longer than that. Their mutual love for Brad had brought them together, and it had grown from there. But had it grown enough? Could he love her? She needed love before they would have a real marriage. She knew that and wasn't about to fool herself.

Bree yawned. "That was fun and a nice way to spend the evening. I'm tired though, and we still have to pick up Lilly in the morning."

"I can pick her up and bring her back by myself." He gave her shoulders a small squeeze.

She shook her head. "No, I want to go with you. I miss her."

"I know. I do, too."

"Well, goodnight. I'll see you in the morning around eight-thirty so we can go get our girl."

He picked up his empty glass. "Sounds good. Goodnight. I'm going to stay up for a while. Maybe watch another movie."

Bree stood. "Okay. Goodnight, again."

Adam stood, too. "Should I walk you to your door, little girl?" He lifted a brow and gave her a grin that would have had female heart's thumping everywhere... if they'd seen it.

As it was, it was just for her, and her heart was the

one pounding in her chest, wishing theirs was a true marriage.

* * *

"Bree."

Knock! Knock! Knock!

"Bree."

She woke up hearing her name and sat straight up. "Lilly?" She shook her head to rid it of the cobwebs left from sleep. A glance at her phone told her it was half-past three in the morning. "What now?" she whispered to herself. She threw back the blankets to get out of bed.

"Bree! Let me in."

"Adam?" She blinked her eyes and again shook her head.

The door suddenly opened wide, and Adam stood in the doorway, turned into a silhouette by the light in the hallway behind him.

"Adam! What are you doing here?"

He stepped into the room and over to the bed.

She wished she could see him. All she could make out was that he was wearing only his boxer shorts.

"I need you, Bree. Do you need me, too? Can you need me, too, just for one night?"

He needs me. He loves me but is afraid to say it. Is it true or is it just my heart wishing for it?

She believed him and lifted her arms to his, opening them wide.

He understood, dropped his boxers, and came to her in the bed, gathering her in his arms. Then he found her lips with his and kissed her. He rolled with her until she was on top of him, then his lips were on her again. Kissing her deeply, urgently.

The kiss made her feel things she hadn't felt in a long time.

She wanted him, and the fact that he loved her made it all right. They were married, after all.

Adam spent the night with her, making love to her several times.

She was worn out but felt well loved.

ADAM WOKE BEFORE BREE. He enjoyed looking at her as she slept and hoped he'd get to see her in the morning every day. She looked like a perfect angel, with her blonde hair forming a halo on the pillow. He wanted to touch her, to make love to her again, but he knew she was probably sore. She hadn't had a boyfriend since Brad, and she wasn't the type to go in for a one-night stand.

He didn't know what she would feel this morning, in the glaring light of day. If Lilly had been there, he would have suggested that all three of them remain in bed for the whole day. But that dream wouldn't happen today. Maybe soon, if he had his way.

* * *

By morning Bree was exhausted and she cuddled next to Adam, weary, but happy.

Adam ran his fingers up and down her arm. "Bree, we have to get up and go get Lilly."

"Ugg. I just want to lie here and rest. I'm tired." Her body ached but in a good way because she knew she'd been loved and made love to.

He chuckled. "I'm glad to see I'm not the only one who's tired today. I have a meeting today but perhaps when Lilly takes a nap, you can, too."

She lay with her head on his chest and her arm draped across his waist, enjoying the feel of his taut warm skin and the muscles that rippled underneath. "That would be nice, but it is not likely to happen. I need to be awake when she wakes up. I don't want her in a wet diaper any longer than necessary."

"Well, we should get up and get showered."

She waggled her eyebrows, not letting her nerves get the better of her. "Do you want to save water and shower together?"

Adam looked away. "Um, I don't think that's a good idea. I don't want you to get the wrong impression."

Bree narrowed her eyes. "And what impression would that be?"

Adam closed his eyes and sighed. "I knew this was a mistake, but I couldn't stay away. We are well and truly married now, but that doesn't mean we are anything more than best friends. You realize that?"

Her chest tightened as she clenched her jaw and narrowed her eyes. He'd used her. He didn't love her at all…not the way she needed and wanted. "Of course. What else would I think? Hmm? Maybe that you were in love with me? But that's ridiculous. You simply had urges and couldn't get them handled any other way because you're married now, right?"

He ran a hand through his hair.

Any other time she might have smiled, but now a smile over anything wasn't in her. Regardless of the fact he looked like a mad professor, with his hair up in all different directions. Today it didn't amuse her.

He turned back toward her with a frown. His nostrils flared. "Oh, don't put it that way. You enjoyed yourself, too. We're married. There's nothing wrong with what we did."

"Right. Nothing wrong." She jumped out of bed. "I'll get Lilly. Why don't you go to work and get to your meeting?"

He took a deep breath. "I can come with you to pickup Lilly. The meeting can wait."

"There is no need for that. I'm perfectly capable of picking up our daughter from her grandparents. Now, I need to shower and prepare to go. You can shower and get dressed for your meeting…in your room." She turned on her heel and headed for her bathroom, leaving Adam with his mouth open.

"This isn't over," he called after her. "Not by a long shot."

"We'll see." She stopped long enough to turn and glare. "We'll see."

CHAPTER 8

ree showered and dressed. Then she picked up her purse and placed the items from her clutch to it.

In the garage, she slid into the driver's seat of the Navigator SUV because Lilly's car seat was already in it, and she didn't have time to transfer it to another vehicle. She told herself she wouldn't look to see if another of Adam's vehicles was gone. But as she backed out of the garage, she couldn't help herself and saw that the Camaro was missing. *Good let him stew and think about what he did.*

By the time Bree reached Madelyn and Rocky's home, she was in a better mood.

Lilly was in her highchair eating Cheerios. Though she had more of the cereal in her hair and on the floor than on her tray or in her mouth, but she was happy.

That was all Bree cared about.

She stopped next to Lilly. "How was my girl? Did she give you any problems?" She kissed the baby's head.

Madelyn, sitting at the table, next to Lilly, waved off her concern. "She was an absolute angel. I've never known such a happy baby. Certainly, none of mine were."

Rocky laughed. He sat at the opposite end of the table with a copy of the Denver Post newspaper. He still hadn't made it to the computer age where he read his news online. He much preferred to have the newspaper in his hands.

"You've got that right. I think all our children were holy terrors, even Megan. And I thought the kid being a girl would be easier. I was wrong. She might have been the worst of them because she was the baby and the only girl. She got spoiled by all of the boys, though none of them will admit it now."

Bree plucked Lilly out of the highchair, brushing the Cheerios off her cheeks and out of her hair. "We need to get going, sweetie. Mommy has a lot to do today."

Madelyn lifted a brow. "What's got you so busy?"

"I'm working on my business plan for the gardening center I hope to open one day. And I need to write while she sleeps. I have a book due to the editor."

"That sounds like the garden center would be right up your alley. You do love your garden. Will you put one in at Adam's house now that it's your house, too?" asked Madelyn.

Bree nodded and then pulled her hair from Lilly's

grasp. "That's the plan. I'm doing flower gardens. Carole already has a vegetable garden. I'll plant the tulip bulbs in the fall, around October, and then everything else in the spring of next year."

Madelyn nodded. "Okay, we won't keep you. I have everything packed in her diaper bag." Madelyn pointed at the bag on a chair at the table.

"Great. Thanks so much for watching her. I hope she wasn't too much trouble."

"She is never trouble. She's our granddaughter, and we love her and love having her here. So, when are you and Adam going to add to your family?"

Bree was blindsided and couldn't speak for a moment. "Umm…what?"

Madelyn cocked her head to the side and clasped her hands in front of her. "You—Adam—children? You are planning to have more, aren't you?"

"Um, well, we really haven't discussed it much. I guess we're waiting to see how well raising Lilly goes. We want to make sure we're good parents before bringing another baby into the family. Besides that, I don't want two children in diapers at the same time. So, it will be years before we decide to have another child."

How do I keep from telling them that will never happen, because a repeat of last night will never happen? Adam doesn't love me and probably never will. Now, I know that and won't fall for the I need you line again. I need you doesn't mean I love you. I must remember that.

Bree buckled Lilly's car seat into the SUV and

headed home. By the time she arrived, the baby had fallen asleep with her pacifier in her mouth. The sight made Bree smile. "I love you so much, little girl. I never believed I could love someone as much as I do you."

Suddenly, she heard a soft knock on her window.

Adam stood there.

Where did he come from? He must have been watching for us.

She opened the door, grabbed her keys, and exited the vehicle. "What do you want?"

He lifted his eyebrows. "I wondered if you wanted me to take our sleeping daughter," he jutted his chin toward Lilly, "into the house." He didn't mention the elephant in the room.

"I could take her inside, but she'll probably stay asleep if you do it. I'll get the diaper bag."

He nodded and proceeded to extricate Lilly from the car seat.

Because they would be downstairs, Adam laid her in the playpen in the family room.

Bree covered her with a light blanket. When she looked up, she saw Adam gazing at her with a smile.

"I want—"

Bree put a finger over her lips. "Shh. Kitchen," she whispered. Even though the kitchen wasn't far away, Lilly was at the far end of the family room, so they could speak normally.

Adam followed her.

Carole had already been there and was nowhere in sight.

"Now, what did you want to say?"

"Just that I want you to move the rest of your things into my room. The bed is much more comfortable than the one you're in now."

"No." She turned away and grabbed a cup from the cupboard over the Keurig coffee maker. Then she took a pod of Earl Grey tea from the revolving holder and put it in the machine. She needed something to calm her nerves, and the hour was too early to drink bourbon.

He crossed his arms over his chest. "No? That's all you have to say?"

"Yes. I won't be moving into your bedroom now or in the foreseeable future. And what do you mean by the rest of my things?"

"Why? I thought, after last night—"

"Last night was a mistake. One that will not be repeated. I should have known you didn't love me, but I was like a schoolgirl and convinced myself you wouldn't have come if you didn't love me. That's on me."

He ran a hand through his hair, then he let out a deep breath. "Bree...I...I thought you understood. There can't be anything more between us than what we have. I do love you...as my best friend. How many people can say they married their best friend?"

"Not many. How many people can say they were screwed over by their best friend? Probably a lot more than anyone wants to admit. You knew I wanted love before having a sexual relationship and yet you took advantage of me. That's not what best friends do."

"Bree…I never meant to take advantage of you. I thought when you opened your arms to me, that you needed me as much as I needed you. I still need you, Bree. I want you. I want to have a true marriage. We have a real marriage; you simply don't want to admit it." Adam stood and paced as he talked. Then he stopped in front of her. "You enjoyed what we did last night as much as I did, don't deny it."

"There is no talking to you. You will never understand." She took her cup of tea to the room they had made into her office. Remembering what Valerie said, she wondered if it was true. Would he never love her? Was he incapable of loving a woman as she needed

Adam picked Lilly up from the playpen and followed Bree. Then he stopped on the other side of the desk from her and held Lilly with one arm around her belly and the other under her bottom. "Most of your things have already been moved. I thought you'd say yes, so I called and instructed Carole to move them after you left to get Lilly."

She set her tea on her desk and then rounded on him. "How could you do that?" Her voice was soft, even though she wanted to scream. "You. Had. No. Right."

"I have every right. You're *my wife*." He thumped his chest. "And I want to sleep next to *my wife*."

"No. I'll just move them back."

He threw his arm out. "And I'll have them moved again. Carole won't want to keep doing it, but I can hire someone whose job is only that and I'll pay them well. They won't leave and they will be loyal to me."

Bree felt her blood boiling. She stood with her hands fisted at her sides. "You can be a real bast—"

He held up an index finger and waved it in front of her face. "No cursing. We agreed not to incase Lilly was listening."

Bree widened her eyes. "She's a baby."

"You agreed."

She narrowed her eyes and flared her nostrils. "Fine, but you know what I was going to say, and it had nothing to do with your birth or your parentage. I happen to love your parents, but they were asking some uncomfortable questions today."

He furrowed his brows. "What kind of questions?"

She shrugged. "Oh, just things like when are we giving Lilly a brother or sister?"

Holding Lilly with one arm, he then ran his free hand back and forth over his hair.

Bree almost laughed because his hair was now sticking up all over. Definitely not the look for a billionaire CEO of one of the biggest holding companies in the world. If he could acquire Danvers, then Kincaid Holdings would be the biggest in the country and maybe the world. She knew he had a lot riding on his acquisition of Danvers. "I married you because I want children. You needed a wife for your acquisition of Danvers. Let's not make it more than it is. A marriage of convenience, nothing more. I won't go looking for another husband. You know I don't believe in divorce, and I won't be separated from Lilly. If you want to seek sex outside of our marriage, do so. You have my permission, but I'd prefer it if you didn't have any more accidents or come home with a disease. That's all I ask." She turned away, sat at her desk, and booted up her computer. She looked up at Adam. "Was there anything else you needed?"

He gritted his teeth. "No."

She saw the anger he was keeping tamped. It showed in his eyes. But she wouldn't back down. He could be as angry with her as he liked, because the only thing she cared about was Lilly. As long as their battle didn't affect her, she was fine with whatever this turned out to be.

The minute it impacted their little girl was the minute she would end it, however that might be.

* * *

BREE LEFT her clothes in Adam's room for the time being. Only taking things for tomorrow and her nightgown and robe for that night. She went into her bathroom and prepared for bed.

When she came back out, she couldn't believe her eyes.

Adam was in her bed, bare chested, with the blankets bunched around his waist. He wore glasses and read a book.

"What do you think you're doing?"

He didn't look up. "Reading."

She snorted. "Not that you ass. What are you doing in my bed?"

He waved a finger. "No cursing. Remember we agreed."

"We agreed to that when Lilly was around." She waved an arm, taking in the entire room.

Adam laid his open book on his lap and looked up. "Well, the mountain won't come to Mohammed, so Mohammed has come to the mountain. You're my wife, and I intend to sleep with my wife. You prefer here, so this is where I'll sleep."

She felt unbelievably frustrated. "You can't be serious." She knew he was, but didn't have any idea how to move him.

He narrowed his eyes and clasped his hands on top of the book. "I am…deadly serious."

"Well, I'm not sleeping here if you are. I'll sleep in your room."

He closed his book and set it on the nightstand. "Good. Let's go." He got out of bed wearing only his boxers.

"Without you." His chest was hard muscle with definite six-pack abs. She knew from cuddling with him last night. She forced herself to look away and concentrate on his eyes.

From the bed, he waved an index finger from side to side. "It doesn't work that way. I'm sleeping with my wife, wherever she sleeps."

Bree closed her eyes and fisted her hands before opening them again. "You are so annoying."

He grinned like a loon. "I know. I've been perfecting it the last couple of years. How do you think I'm doing? Too annoying? Not enough? I want to make sure it's just right."

"You are always too much."

He walked over and stood in front of her. Soft hands pushed an errant strand of hair behind her ear. "I would prefer not to be, but I have no choice. You haven't given me a choice in the matter. What if you're already pregnant? What then? You know I'll never let you go, don't you?"

"And I told you, I don't believe in divorce, so we would raise this child together. If you find someone else to marry, after the fact, you'll have to decide what you really want. I will never give up my child. I'm not Sally."

He clenched his jaw, then relaxed it. "I won't ever want to marry someone else. I know you're not Sally. You're not Valerie either. I don't believe you'll ever cheat on me." Adam ran a finger down her cheek and gave her a wan smile. "You don't want me for my money and that makes me happy."

No. I don't want you for your money, but I want you very much. I want your love.

"Why did you really marry me, Bree?"

If only you knew how much I love you and have for the last two years, you would never have married me.

She pulled her head away from him and looked away. "I wanted a child. You know that I told you so. And you were my only way to get it."

Adam shook his head and crossed his arms, showing off his muscled biceps. "You could have adopted. There are lots of children to adopt."

Bree bit her lower lip before she spoke. "I suppose I could have, and perhaps we still will."

He lifted his brows and widened his eyes. "Why should we adopt when we can have children of our own?"

"You know why. I'm not having sex with you again. It was a mistake, and I believe you took advantage of me."

Adam waved his arm in dismissal. "Oh, don't go there. You know you enjoyed what we did. You didn't care at that moment whether I loved you or not. You were just as glad as I was not to be alone." He paced away and back again. Stopping in front of her, he reached out .

She stepped back.

"You know as well as I do that you don't want to sleep alone." He reached out and cupped her cheek. "I just want to hold you. Nothing else will happen. I promise and when have you ever known me not to keep a promise?"

"Never. You always keep your promises."

"This isn't any different—no that's not true. This is more important because I'm making the promise to you, and I will keep it…even if it kills me."

A laugh burst forth from Bree. "Oh, sorry. I don't know why that is funny, but something about the way you said it struck my funny bone." She stopped and wiped her eyes, errant tears lurking there. "I believe you, Adam. I want to trust you and, for the most part, I do. It's me I don't trust. Me that I have to guard against."

"You're right, because if you come to me all warm and cuddly and want to make love, I will be happy to accommodate you."

She looked down. "I know, and I'll be happy about it in the moment and feeling stupid about it afterwards."

He took her left hand in his and worried her wedding ring with his thumb. "You should never feel stupid after we make love. Never. We're married now, Bree. I'm not sure what the future holds for us, but I hope it's more children. You *do* remember how we get more children, don't you?"

She rolled her eyes so far back in her head she should have fallen backwards with the movement. "I know how to make children; I just didn't see it as a future for us." She headed down to the kitchen.

Adam followed her, apparently eschewing clothes. "Honey, I didn't either, but we can make the future what we want."

"Not without love. I can't do it. I know you don't understand, but I need what I need, and that's to be loved, wholly and completely."

Adam dropped her hand. "You know I can't do that. I refuse to let myself get into that situation again."

She sat on one of the barstools at the kitchen's island. "I know. I was there when that…witch…did what she did. You don't have to feel that was all on you.

She never loved you. She loved your money. It's a good thing you had the prenup, or she would have taken you to the cleaners. There's something else I should tell you." She wrung her hands. "Brad said I should mind my own business, but I wish I hadn't taken his advice."

His eyebrows furrowing, he sat next to her and took her hand again. "What? You can tell me anything, Bree."

"Okay. I knew Valerie was having an affair with Simon, even before you married. I'm sorry, I should have told you, but Brad said it wasn't our business."

Adam dropped her hand. "You knew. I thought you were my friend."

"Dang it, I am your friend. I…I hoped she was ending it with Simon when I heard you were getting married. I didn't find out she hadn't until after the wedding, and by then it was too late. Besides, you were besotted with her. Would you even have believed me?"

His shoulders slumped, and he shook his head. "You're right, I wouldn't have. I would have thought it was some weird form of jealousy."

She reached over to touch his arm.

He pulled away. "I think I'll get dressed and go for a drive. I need to figure some things out."

She stood straighter, her back as stiff as if she had a steel rod up it. "Fine. I'm going to check on Lilly. And Adam? Don't come back until you have your head on straight."

Bree slipped around him before he could see the tears in her eyes and headed up the stairs.

He followed her up.

She heard the door to his bedroom slam, followed just minutes later by the door to the garage. Bree knew he was leaving until he wasn't angry any longer. What would happen when he got back…she had no idea.

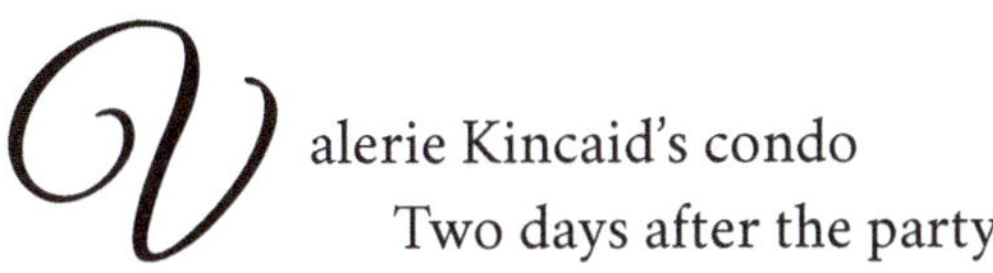

alerie Kincaid's condo
Two days after the party

"What do you mean you hit her? Why in the world would you do that, Valerie? If the Danvers find out, you have as good as assured that Kincaid's bid will be accepted over mine." Simon Chandler lashed out with his left hand and backhanded her.

Valerie fell to the floor and crawled over to him, wrapping her arms around his legs and looking up. "I'm sorry, Master. It will never happen again. I'll make nice with her. I promise, it will be okay."

Simon placed a palm on her upturned face and pushed her away.

"Please, Master, let me fix this."

"I don't think you can. Leave me, now."

She bowed as she backed away. "Yes, Master."

Stupid woman. If she didn't satisfy other needs, I would get rid of her, but she is so good at being submissive, and I enjoy her too much. But what she did will set back my efforts. I thought I had it in the bag until Kincaid showed up with his perfect wife. I hadn't realized how good Bree Taylor was or I might have married her myself. Now I have to see if I can fix what my submissive likely cost me and I'm not sure how to go about it.

SUNDAY, two days after the party and the disastrous aftermath, Bree was in a good mood as she fed Lilly her jar of baby food.

Lilly liked the pureed peas and even more wanted to play with the spoon Bree was using to feed her. She kept grabbing for the spoon .

But Bree was faster, keeping it out of Lilly's hands.

Adam appeared in the kitchen, going over to Lilly and kissing the top of her head. "How are my two favorite girls this morning?"

Bree looked up and smiled. "We are doing great. She's eating her peas and trying to grab the spoon. We're having a typical day. I think I'll let her play on the floor in the living room with a wooden spoon and a couple of pans. She'll like that, even if it will be noisy for us." Bree was wearing yoga pants and a huge Colorado University Buffaloes t-shirt along with Nike sneakers. She knew better than to wear nice clothes when feeding Lilly her baby food. It got literally everywhere.

Adam grabbed a coffee pod and placed it in the Keurig machine. "That will be fun for her and won't bother me. I'll be ensconced in my office all morning."

"Working on the Danvers proposal?"

He nodded. "Thanks to you I think we have a good shot at him accepting my offer. I don't believe Simon can come up with something better, but stranger things have happened."

"If they knew what Valerie did to me in the bathroom, then you would definitely have a lock on it. But I didn't want to be the one to make trouble for you."

He added sugar to his coffee and took a sip. "You didn't do anything wrong. You were perfect, and they loved you."

"I really liked them, too." She took another spoonful of peas and made *choo-choo* noises. "Here comes the train. Open the tunnel."

Lilly giggled and opened her mouth.

Bree put the spoon in her mouth, smoothing it on the top of Lilly's palate to make sure she got the whole spoonful. She did this a couple more times before Lilly turned away and shook her head.

"Looks like our little girl is full."

"Yes, and she needs cleaning up and a diaper change. Would you do that while I take care of her highchair? I'm afraid not all of the peas went in her mouth."

"Of course." He set his coffee on the counter. Then

he went to Lilly, unfastened the safety belt and lifted her from the highchair. "Good gawd. From the looks of her I'm surprised she got any in her mouth."

"She was very messy today and managed to grab the spoon a couple of times." Bree raised her brows and pursed her lips. Then she took the highchair tray to the sink. "That's why it's in her hands and hair. Maybe you should just give her a bath and start the morning over."

Adam held Lilly at arm's length, lest he be wearing peas, too. "I think that's probably a good idea. From the smell of her that will be the best way for everything to get clean."

Bree laughed at the picture they made. The big man and the little baby. She looked almost tiny in his arms. "You might as well get used to the idea that you'll have to change your shirt after you're done."

He looked at the sleeves of his shirt, which were smeared with baby handprints made of peas, and sighed, bringing Lilly fully into his arms and against his chest. "You, my darling daughter, are a messy eater. I hope you grow out of that as you get older."

"We can only hope," said Bree from the kitchen sink, where she was using the sprayer to rinse the tray. Then she grabbed a dishtowel from the first drawer on the left side of the sink and dried the tray. She set it on the table and wiped down the vinyl chair.

Adam carried Lilly upstairs for a bath and clean clothes.

Bree admired that Adam was a hands-on dad. He could have left her to care for Lilly completely. But he was a great father. He wanted to be involved in all aspects of Lilly's care, and Bree let him. She was perfectly happy not to have to deal with every dirty diaper, though she missed giving her a bath. They'd purchased a little ring that suctioned onto the tub where Lilly could sit in and play.

She loved her bath time. She splashed and played and chewed on everything she could get her hands on.

She was teething and drooling like a St. Bernard dog. Her clothes were often wet, and she had to be changed.

Bree had gotten to where she kept a bib on Lilly all the time, just to keep her clothes drier.

She was watching Adam give Lilly a bath when the doorbell rang. Bree got up to go answer it.

Adam looked up at her. "Carole will get it, so you don't have to leave."

"Carole is at the grocery store. I need to answer the door. Besides it's probably the florist. I decided to get some new plants for the formal dining table. I like to keep fresh ones in there. That new girl, Camile, you have working for you in the acquisitions department told me about this florist and that they were having a great plant sale. I called and ordered several things and gave them the code for the gate."

"Oh, okay. I'll have Lilly out of the bath and in the nursery by the time you return."

"I'll look for you there." She walked downstairs and reached the front door just as the doorbell sounded again. She opened the door. "How may I hel—"

A burly man in a ski mask stood on the porch with a gun. "Don't make a sound. Come with us, and the man and baby won't be harmed."

Bree looked up at where Adam would be with Lilly and knew she didn't have a choice. "Let me get my purse." She wondered how many men there were since the one with the gun had said *us*. She heart pounded and she wondered if she'd ever see Adam or Lilly again.

"No. No purse. No phone. Just you."

She nodded. "Fine."

He led the way to a white van that said *Sandy's Floral* on the side, opened the sliding door, and jutted his chin at the opening. "Get in."

She'd stepped up to enter the van.

The man gave her a hard push.

"Hurry up!"

She was pushed into the van, landing on her right side.

Then the man slid the door closed and as soon as he was in the passenger's side, the driver took off before the masked man even had his door shut.

"Where are you taking me?"

"Some place safe. You don't need to worry."

Bree knew she needed to make the men afraid. Maybe they didn't know the penalty for what they were doing. Maybe she could bluff her way to getting them to believe that Adam cared enough to get her back. "Who are you working for? Why did you kidnap me? That's a federal offense you know. You're in big trouble. When my husband finds out what you've done, he'll come after you and he won't stop until he finds me. He'll kill you for what you've done. I hope whatever you're getting paid is enough to be worth your life."

"Shut it, before I kill you now."

The driver, who was also masked, looked at the man in the passenger's side. "Do you think she's right?"

The man shrugged. "It's doesn't matter now. What's done is done."

The driver looked at the burly man. "You didn't tell me we could go to jail."

"Oh, puuleeease." Bree stretched out the word and rolled her eyes, even though neither man had eyes on her. "You're kidnapping me. What did you think would happen? Did you think the police would just give you a candy bar, and it would all be okay?"

"No," snapped the driver. "I never thought we'd be caught."

"And we won't be. We're just supposed to drop her off at the agreed upon location and leave her there. Then we get to go back to our lives with lots of money and forget this ever happened,"

"You're fools if you believe that. Whoever hired you won't want to leave any witnesses, and you are definitely witnesses."

"Mr. Chandler would never do that," said the driver. He looked at the first man. "Would he? Joe, would he?"

Joe, the first man, didn't answer the question, but he hit the driver in the shoulder. "You idiot. Now, she knows my name...*Calvin*."

"That's just mean. I did it by accident. I didn't mean to tell her, you did it on purpose. What are we gonna do now?"

"We stick with the plan. There's nothing more we can do. Just drive."

"Fine." Calvin turned his attention to the highway

She was glad for it because all the weaving and rolling around in the back on the metal floor wasn't comfortable on her backside. *I'll be very glad to get out of this van...unless they decide to kill me instead.*

* * *

ADAM CARRIED Lilly down to the kitchen. "Bree," he called as he walked into the room.

But Bree wasn't there. He proceeded throughout the house. "Bree? Where are you? Bree."

"Adam! Adam!" yelled Carole

He found Carol in the kitchen.

"Adam she's gone. Someone took her."

"What do you mean 'took her'?"

"I just got home, and I thought I saw a man put her in the back of a van. I was just calling 911."

"Continue. While you do that, I'm calling my security people." He gripped Lilly tighter.

The baby fussed and tried to pull away.

He eased his grip. "I'm sorry, Sweetheart. Daddy is just scared for Mommy, but we'll get her back." He turned his gaze toward Carole. "I don't care what it costs, we will get her back."

Carole nodded as she placed her call to 911 and described the van and the man to the best of her ability.

Adam repeated to his man what Carole said.

When she was done, she ended the call. "The police will put out an APB, but I don't have a lot of hope they'll find it."

"Why not?"

"Because the man knew the code to the gate and knew we were getting flowers today. How could they know those things?"

"I don't know. It sounds like I have a spy in my organization. Bree mentioned one of my new employees, someone named Camile, gave her the tip about this florist. I'll have Camile picked up before she has a chance to flee." Adam put Lilly in her playpen.

She immediately picked up a teething ring and began chewing on it.

He turned back toward his housekeeper. "Don't give up yet. My men will find her. They have contacts even I can't imagine."

Carole stood wringing her hands in front of her. "I hope so. I just wish I'd come back five minutes sooner; this wouldn't have happened. I would have been the one to answer the door and—"

"You can't think that way. You couldn't have done anything to change it. For those men to take her, in broad daylight, like they did, they were probably desperate, and you might have been injured or killed if you'd gotten in their way." Adam placed an arm around her shoulders. "Don't worry, we'll find her. I won't stop until I do. Nothing is as important to me as Bree and Lilly." He squeezed her shoulders. "I need to ask a favor of you. Will you take care of Lilly for me? I need to go to the office to coordinate the search. It's much easier to do it from there where we have all the equipment needed."

She looked up at him. "Of course, I'll take care of her. I'll protect her with my life."

"I hope that will never happen. Keep all the doors locked and don't open them for anyone but me. Even then I'll come in through the garage. Set the alarm system after I leave. I can monitor it from work."

"I will. I promise." Carole's mouth formed a flat line. "I'll lock the front door now."

"Good. I need to say goodbye to Lilly."

Carole nodded and left to do her errand.

Adam stalked to the playpen and picked up Lilly. "Sweetheart, I have to leave for a while. Auntie Carole will be here and taking care of you. I have to go get your mommy back." He kissed her forehead.

She slapped his face with her wet left hand and a slobber-covered teething ring in her right hand.

Both seemed sticky, too, but he couldn't figure out from what. It didn't matter. He kissed her again and returned her to the playpen.

Lilly began to cry.

Carole came into the room from the kitchen behind him. "Don't worry about her. I'll make sure she's okay." She picked up Lilly.

The baby stopped crying and grinned at Carole.

The woman laughed.

Adam wanted to, as well, but the thought of being unable to share it with Bree dampened his mirth. He hurried out of the kitchen to the six-car garage, got in the Corvette, and drove to his downtown Denver office.

His office was in a thirty-two story building known as The Kincaid Tower. His office was on the thirty-first floor. The thirty-second floor was an open area with two bars, several seating areas with beige couches and dark brown leather chairs.

The elevator opened directly to his administrative assistant, Emily's desk.

Emily looked up.

"All the men are here and ready to report to you."

"Thank you. Hold my calls unless it's about Bree."

"Of course." Emily went back to her work.

Adam entered his office and saw his three top security employees waiting. Two were in the chairs directly in front of his desk. The third was on the sofa on the right side of the room. Adam sat behind his desk.

"Tell me what you have. Jesse, you first."

Jesse was a dark-haired man with a Van Dyke beard. He looked down at the tablet in his lap. "We pulled traffic footage and found the white van as it was leaving your neighborhood. We tracked it until it stopped in an industrial area. Two men got out of the van, and they had a woman with them. The people went inside a warehouse owned by Simon Chandler.

Seven minutes later the two men returned to the van and drove away. "

Adam slammed his fist on his desk and leaned back in his chair. "This has something to do with the Danvers account. Simon wants it, and he's taken Bree to stop me from getting it by making me back off."

The blond, clean-shaven man sitting next to the dark-haired man crossed his right leg on his left knee. "I believe we can free her. It appeared that the men just dropped her off and left. The van was tracked back to a flower shop where the men abandoned it and got into a black SUV."

Adam stood and paced behind his desk. He stopped and stared at the blond man. "Well, Sid, did you track the SUV?"

Sid shook his head. "We figured we should keep an eye on the warehouse where Bree is."

"You're right. That's the important thing." Adam looked at the third man. He had dark, curly hair that was almost black. His skin was olive, he had a small gold hoop earring in his left ear and a plain gold wedding band on his left ring finger. "What do you think, Tony?"

Tony sat up, then placed his elbows on his knees, and clasped his hands together. "I think we need to act like Seal Team 6 and get Bree out of there before Simon hurts her. You and I both know what Simon is capable of."

Adam's stomach clenched. He didn't like the thought of killing someone, but Bree came first. He'd do what was necessary. "I want to do it as soon as possible. And I'm going with you. Just because I'm not a SEAL anymore, doesn't mean I've lost my skills."

"Adam are you sure you want to do that? You have a baby at home now to think of. What if something happens to you and Bree?" asked Jesse.

Turning his attention toward Jesse, Adam ran his hands through his hair. "I have to be there…for Bree. I can't explain it. I just know I have to be there."

Jesse threw up his hands. "Okay, let's do this."

CHAPTER 10

The four men rode the elevator to the basement. The only way to get there was with Adam's palm print.

The doors opened directly into a large room whose walls were covered with racks of guns. AR-15, Uzis, Glock handguns, and several different kinds of long rifles. One wall held other tools of combat. Things like knives, grenades and bayonets for the rifles.

Another wall was full of ammunition for each of the weapons.

Each man picked out a bullet proof vest and then another vest to hold ammo and grenades. They each grabbed the guns they were most familiar with.

Adam picked up two Glocks, a side holster and a rifle. The first gun he holstered on his side and the second pistol he put in the back of his waistband. He placed a knife on his belt and then filled his vest with ammo for the Glocks and the rifle.

The other three men did the same, choosing their favorite weapons.

The men were loaded for bear, and they weren't looking at taking any prisoners.

When all were done, Adam led them back to the private garage and a waiting black panel van.

Tony slid behind the wheel with Adam in the passenger seat.

The other two men sat in back, one on either side of the van, on the bench seats specially installed there.

This van was not for delivering flowers but for delivering men. Armed men.

Simon would know Adam's wrath. No one took what belonged to him...without paying the consequences.

* * *

Bree waited in the enormous warehouse, empty except for the wooden chair she was tied to and another one directly in front of her. She continued to wait, for she didn't know what. While she did, she worked on getting her hands loose, but since they were behind her, she wasn't having much luck.

She had to admit, even to herself, she was scared and wished Adam was there. He would keep the monsters at bay. And he would make whoever did this pay.

A door opened behind her, and she heard the thud of boot steps coming toward her.

"Well, if it isn't the pretty Mrs. Adam Kincaid."

Simon Chandler. Why wasn't she surprised?

He walked around so he faced Bree. "Welcome, Mrs. Kincaid. Or can I call you Bree?"

She lifted her chin. "Mrs. Kincaid, if you please. Only my friends call me Bree and you're definitely not my friend."

He came closer and pinched her chin between the thumb and index finger of his right hand, lifting so she would look at him. "Don't force me to hurt you...*Bree.*"

She pulled her chin free from his fingers and shook back her hair that had fallen forward. "You'll do that if you want to. I think you'll get off on it just like Valerie does. Tell me that's not why you keep her around? Janie wouldn't play your games, so you found Valerie. It didn't matter that Adam fell in love with her, that made it all the sweeter, didn't it?"

Simon scoffed. "You know a lot for just being Kincaid's wife."

While she continued to subtly work on her hands, Bree lifted her chin. "I knew Valerie in college, and I knew you were seeing her before she married Adam. I'd hoped she was in love with Adam, would make him a good wife and would end it with you. I didn't know, until I saw you together at the Danvers' party, that she only married him under your orders."

Simon laughed. "Of course, it was under orders, and it worked...for a while."

"Yes, until he caught you two together. Why on earth would you do it at their house?"

He shrugged. "Yes, that was stupid on my part. I thought Adam was at work and, believe it or not, I missed her."

Bree nodded. "Right. You missed her. I don't believe that for a moment. You thought you'd have one more thing to hold over Adam's head. One more thing to torture him with."

Simon moved the other chair, so the back faced Bree. Then he straddled it. He watched her face for hints that she knew what was going on. "You'll only be here for a short time. I'm sure Adam will pay my price."

She continued to work the ropes holding her hands together. The rope cut into her wrists, the burn painful, but not enough to stop her. "Adam won't pay anything for me. Our marriage is one of convenience, not a love match." At least not for him. He could get another woman to be Lilly's mother after Bree was dead. She had no doubt that he could find a willing volunteer. He was too kind and too handsome to be a widower for long. Her throat felt full of the lump that formed there as she thought about Adam with another woman.

"Ah, poor Bree, she doesn't even realize Adam's in love with her. He's been in love with you for years. I think even before he divorced Valerie, though I'm not sure he recognized it. He was always there for you. Whenever you needed him, he dropped whatever he was doing and ran to your aid."

Her heart jumped into her throat and her pulse raced. *Could it be true?* "That's not true. He loved Valerie. That's why he married her."

He slashed a hand out. "Don't be naïve. He thought it was time he married and did so with the woman he was currently dating. That was Valerie. On my orders, of course."

"How do you know so much about Adam and what he's feeling? I didn't know you were close."

"We used to be. He and I worked together for some time before he started Kincaid Holdings. I thought we'd start it together, but then I made the mistake of going after one of the accounts on my own. He found out and that was the end of our working together."

"Sounds to me like you weren't working together at all. How long did you work behind his back?"

Simon laughed. "You're not only beautiful but smart. Adam's a lucky man."

"I think I'm the lucky one in our marriage."

He waved his hand dismissing her thoughts.

The ropes were loosening, so she kept at it and talked to keep Simon occupied so he didn't notice her working the ropes. He was too proud of himself. "You're an evil man, Simon Chandler. Has anyone ever told you that…to your face?"

He threw back his head and roared with laughter. "You are truly a delight. It's too bad I didn't see you first."

"As if there is anything you could offer to make me be with you."

"You never know. I might just have something, maybe money…"

"I don't need your money. I didn't marry Adam for

his money. I have more money than I'll ever spend. I wanted a family, and I got one. I love Lilly more than my life, so there is nothing you can give me that I don't already have." She removed her left hand from the rope.

His lips turned up on one side. "Perhaps I should have taken the baby instead of you."

She launched herself at him, her hands going for his neck. "You stay away from my daughter. You'll never touch her." She dug her nails into his flesh.

He was stronger than she was and forced her hands away.

She scratched him deeply on both sides of his neck.

He freed his right hand, formed a fist, and slammed it into her jaw.

The impact was enough to shove her off of him.

Simon threw the chair to his right and scrambled to his feet.

Bree laid on her side, the wind knocked out of her.

He kicked her twice in her ribs. "That will teach you to attack me."

Knowing he would kick her again; she made herself as small as possible and bent into a fetal position.

The door to the warehouse blasted open, and four masked men swarmed inside.

One of them ran ahead of the others toward Simon.

He wasn't fast enough to realize what was happening and turned too late to run.

The masked man slammed the butt of his rifle into the side of Simon's face.

Simon spun halfway around and then fell to the floor.

Rushing toward Bree, the masked man crouched beside her.

She felt his fingers on her neck as he checked for her pulse.

"Bree?" He pulled off his mask.

His face swam into view. "Adam? But how?"

"You're going to be okay. The ambulance will be here soon."

Behind him she saw two of the other men pull Simon to his feet. The third man cuffed his wrists behind his back.

"What are you doing here?"

"I came after my wife. No one takes what's mine." His voice softened, and he smiled. Then he tucked a strand of hair behind her ear. "I couldn't let him take Lilly's mother, now, could I?"

Lilly's mother. That's all she was to him. She guessed that was good.

"Her mother. Thank you for coming after me. I don't know how you did it, but I don't care. I'm just glad you're here. Help me up."

Instead of giving her a hand, he slipped his arms under her back and legs, then lifted her high against his chest. Then he kissed her forehead.

She cried at the tenderness he showed, knowing it was only because she was Lilly's mother. Bree loved him, and no help was to be had on that front, so she lay in his arms and cried. Let him think it was her body's injuries and not her soul crying out in pain.

By the time they made it outside, the ambulance was waiting for her.

The police had custody of Simon and were reading him his rights.

Adam carefully placed her on the gurney. "I'll ride with her, if that's okay."

The female paramedic, who had blonde hair in a thick braid falling to her waist, shook her head. "We'd prefer it if you follow in your private vehicle."

Adam frowned but nodded. Then he took Bree's hand. "I'll be right behind you. I won't leave you alone at the hospital."

"I'm all right. You should be home with Lilly."

"Carole has her. I'll text to let her know what's going on. Lilly is in good hands."

Bree tried to smile, but her jaw hurt like Hades, and she grimaced, instead. "Carole loves Lilly almost as much as we do. She'll take good care of her."

The paramedics lifted the gurney into the ambulance and pulled away, headed for the hospital without lights and siren, since she wasn't in danger of dying.

"Where are you taking me?" Bree didn't open her eyes. The weight of what happened to her was too much and she would cry if they were open.

"The closest hospital is Presbyterian St. Lukes, so you'll be going there."

"That's fine. Can you tell if my husband is following?"

The male paramedic who had brown hair, cut short, with whitewalls around the ears, looked behind them. "If he's in a big black van, then yes, he's following."

"That would probably be him," said Bree.

The ride to the hospital seemed to take a long time but was probably only twenty minutes or so.

Bree felt every bump, and the railroad tracks nearly killed her. She was fairly certain she had a couple of broken ribs, thanks to Simon Chandler and his misguided need to win. But he would pay. He'd be going to jail for this. Kidnapping was a federal crime, add battery to the charge and he'd be going away for many years. She figured Janie would throw a party and finally divorce him.

When they arrived at the hospital, Bree was wheeled into the Emergency Room.

Adam came in after her, but he only saw her a minute before the doctor threw him out.

Doctor Strauss was a young man, maybe thirty-five or so, with brown hair, blue eyes and a charming smile. He took her hand in his. "How are you feeling? Can you tell me your name?"

"I'm Bree Kincaid. The man you threw out was my husband, Adam Kincaid. He'll be very angry." For some inexplicable reason, she wanted to laugh. She managed to get out a chuckle before her ribs screamed again. "It feels like my ribs shift with every breath I take."

"I would bet you have, at least, cracked several ribs

and have possibly broken some. I'm getting X-rays done so we know for sure, although the treatment is the same."

"Which is what?"

"Nothing. We can't do anything. We used to wrap them but discovered that can do more damage than good, so we do nothing and let them heal on their own. You'll probably want to sit up in bed to keep the movement as little as possible. Do you have children?"

Bree smiled when she thought of her precious Lilly. "We have an eight-month-old daughter."

The doctor took his stethoscope from around his neck and put it in his ears. "I'm going to listen for fluid in your lungs. I want to rule out a punctured lung."

He listened to her back and then to her chest. "I don't hear anything, so that is good. You won't be able to pick up your daughter for about six weeks. I know it will be hard, but you really need to do it. Your ribs should heal in that time. Pain management is crucial for the first few days up to the first week. I'll be prescribing very strong pain medication, so you'll probably spend most of the time sleeping, which is good."

Her ribs hurt when she breathed but she couldn't help the panic she felt. She was almost in a sitting position on the hospital bed. She figured it was up as far as it would go. The antiseptic smell nearly gagged her. She hated the smell of a hospital. "What about my daughter? How am I supposed to take care of her?"

"I happen to know that your husband can afford a

nanny for that time. Everything will be fine. Let's start with the X-rays." He patted her hand. "I'll be back after I get the test results. In the meantime, I've ordered you some pain medication." He looked up as the curtain around her bed opened to allow a nurse entry. He patted Bree's hand again. "All will be well. You'll see."

The doctor left.

The woman was black, with very dark skin and her hair was in mini-braids all over her head. She was quite lovely, with the most expressive dark brown, almond-shaped eyes.

She signed into the computer and then turned to Bree. "Hi, my name is Timony and I'll be taking care of you until they move you to a room or release you." She snapped a pair of gloves from the box on the wall and put them on. Then she picked up the needle she'd placed on the rolling silver tray. "This is a shot of morphine, Mrs. Kincaid. It will help you with your pain." She put the medication directly into the IV line. "You should feel better in a few minutes."

"Thank you." Suddenly, tears ran down her cheeks. "I'm sorry, I don't know what's the matter with me."

"You've been seriously injured, you're separated from your husband, and generally feeling sorry for yourself, with reason. You shouldn't feel shame at shedding a few tears."

"Thanks, Timony. I needed to hear that."

The woman waved off the thanks. "Sure, hon. Now, I'll get your husband and bring him back. Apparently, he's been somewhat of a bear, pacing and shouting at people. Luckily, we're professionals and don't take um…stuff…off of anyone." She left.

Several minutes later, Adam threw back the curtain. "Bree, sweetheart, are you all right? Are they treating you well? I'll have a talk—"

She frowned. *Why does he sound like he cares more than usual, and what is with calling me sweetheart?* "Adam, shh. I'm going to be fine. The doctor thinks I have a couple of cracked ribs, but he doesn't believe anything else is wrong. If he's right and I do, then we'll need to hire a nanny for the next six to eight weeks—"

He bent over. "You, shh." Then he placed his lips against hers.

She suddenly felt like she could take on the world single-handed. Bree lifted her arms to put them around his neck and immediately dropped them back to the bed as her body howled with pain. "Oww, damnit. Forgive me for cussing, but dang that hurts."

"Knock, knock. Mrs. Kincaid?"

"Yes, I'm Bree Kincaid."

A pretty red-haired woman entered. She had freckles across the bridge of her nose and was clearly used to garnering attention. She had big blue eyes that she perused Adam with before turning to Bree. "I'm Savannah, and I'll be taking you to X-ray. You don't have to do a thing. I'll get all these wires unhooked, and I'll take you right on the gurney. How's that sound?"

"Much better than trying to get up."

"I thought so." She turned to Adam. "Are you Mr. Kincaid?"

"Yes."

"You can have a seat there." She pointed at the two plastic chairs along one side of the curtains. "We'll be back in about forty-five minutes."

"I'll be here." He leaned over and kissed Bree again.

Her eyes widened. "Who are you and what have you done with my husband?"

Adam laughed. "We'll talk later. You go with Savannah now, and I'll be here when you get back. I promise."

CHAPTER 11

When Bree returned from having X-rays taken, she saw Adam was waiting.

He stood as she rolled into the room. "How did it go?"

"It was painful. I had to move for them to get all the X-rays and that hurt like the dickens. I'm better now. And soon, they'll have me hooked back up to the morphine drip."

"Good. I don't like to see you in pain."

The doctor chose that moment to arrive. "Well, Bree." He stopped and looked at Adam. "Mr. Kincaid, I assume."

Adam stepped forward and held out his hand. "I'm Adam Kincaid, Bree's husband. What did the X-rays show?"

"Bree has three broken ribs. I was hoping they were just cracked but they were broken. It will be a long, painful recovery, but we'll try to keep her as comfortable as possible while she's here. I'd like to keep her overnight. I'll send her home with a prescription for shots and tablets for pain relief. If you can't give her the shots, I suggest you hire a nurse to—",

"I'll be taking care of her. If someone will show me how to give the shots, then I can handle it."

Bree stared at Adam. She couldn't believe what he just said. He would take care of her. "But what about your business? Don't you have to go into the office?"

"I'll use couriers to transfer important documents to the main office. Besides someone needs to take care of Lilly and I'd prefer it not be a nanny."

"Um. Okay. I agree it would be better if it were one of us."

Adam turned to the doctor. "There, you see? It will all work out okay."

The doctor nodded. "She's due for a shot. I'll send Timony back in and you can watch her as she gives her the shot."

True to his word, Timony entered the small room. "I'm glad you're here, Mr. Kincaid. This is how to give her the injection. Bree, I need you to roll to your side just a bit so I can inject this in your bottom."

Bree rolled just a little, the pain making her stop. She hoped it was far enough because she didn't want to move again.

"That's good. Now you simply put the needle into the fat part of the bottom. Don't hesitate while doing it because that will hurt Bree. Once the needle is all the way in and press the plunger all the way until it stops.

Hold it for a few seconds and then remove the needle and press a cotton square over the spot for about twenty seconds to make sure there is no blood." She removed the cotton and smiled. "All good. You can roll back now."

Bree moved and couldn't stop the moan. "Oh, God, that hurts."

"It's okay." Timony placed the used needle into the red box and the cotton square into the trash. "You did fine, and you'll feel much better soon. I promise. We'll be transferring you to a private room in just a little while. Your husband arranged it. I'll see you soon." She left.

He furrowed his brows. "How are you feeling? Really."

"Like I was kicked in the ribs and had a fist smashed into my face. How do you think I feel?" She was cranky, she hurt, and she didn't give a fat rat's behind if he knew it. "You said we were going to talk. Now's as good a time as any. So, talk."

"Now isn't a good time. You're in pain and I don't believe you're ready to hear what I have to say."

"Hmpft. I think you don't really want to talk to me."

Adam's eyes twinkled, and his mouth quirked up at the corners. "You're very combative when you hurt. I understand that, and that's another reason I'm not ready to talk. We'll talk when you get home and can see Lilly. I'm sure she misses you."

Tears filled Bree's eyes. "I won't even be able to hug her when I see her, and I can't hold her. She won't understand, and she'll hate me." The tears flowed in earnest now.

"She won't hate you. I'll make sure she sees you every day, and you can kiss her and love on her while I hold her. It will be okay. I promise."

She shook her head. "You can't promise that. She's too little to understand anything but Mommy doesn't want her."

I really need to buy a child-rearing book and make him read it. "That's not what she'll think. We might be surprised at what she understands. If we explain that Mommy's hurt, she might understand. She is getting older now. She's almost nine months, after all."

"She's still a baby. She won't understand why I can't hold her and comfort her. It's going to be a nightmare." Bree wanted to cry again but refused to give in to her mood.

"Bree, sweetheart, I promise it won't be that bad." He gently pushed her hair back behind her ears. "You'll still get to hug her and kiss her and make sure she knows you love her."

She looked at Adam. He was so handsome, and he knew it. What was he doing with her? Why had he been so quick to choose her? And why did he keep calling her sweetheart? Was it because she was injured?

Timony picked that moment to come back in. "Time to take you to your room. How are you feeling? That shot should have taken effect by now."

Bree nodded. "I do feel better...as long as I don't move." She grinned then remembered her conversation with Adam. "Do you know when I'll be able to lift my baby?"

"How old is he?"

"She's nine-months-old."

Timony smiled and touched Bree's arm. "She's at the point where she's very squirmy and moves a lot. You can't handle that without beaucoup pain. It would be best if you didn't even try until the doctor says you can."

"All right. Thank you," said Adam.

Timony unhooked the blood pressure cuff and took the oxygen meter off her finger. The IV stand was attached to the bed so she didn't need to unhook the IV from Bree. Then Timony pulled the bed out of the curtained-off room and began to push it.

Adam walked behind her. "How will you get her into the bed in the room?"

"Another nurse or nurse's assistant, a CNA, will be there to help me. We'll literally grab the sheet she's on and pull it across onto the other bed. We can't have her trying to get up yet, that includes to use the restroom. She'll have to use a bedpan."

"I just want her to have the best care possible."

Timony answered him. "Trust me, Mr. Kincaid, we give all of our patients the best care possible, whether they can pay or not. You obviously can pay, but that doesn't mean the care she will receive is better than it would be for someone who is unable to."

Bree could hear the disdain in her voice.

Adam held up his hands in front of himself. "I

realize that. I didn't mean to disparage you or your fellow nurses and CNAs."

Timony shrugged. "It's all right. Most people make the same assumption—that money equals better care. It doesn't—all it gives you is a better room."

"I'm okay with that," said Adam.

The room she rolled Bree into was plain. A bed, small dresser, recliner, a silver rolling tray and a roll-away tray to go over the bed were the only pieces of furniture. A TV hung on the wall in front of the bed. The room did have a view of the mountains, which was nice.

A young brunette woman waited in the room.

"This is Ginger," said Timony. "She and I are going to slide you over to the bed. You just lay there and don't try to help. It will only make it more difficult for you and for us. Understand?"

Bree nodded. "Got it. Don't help."

Timony unhooked Bree from the IV. Then she and Ginger moved to the opposite side of the bed, leaned over and grabbed the sheet Bree lay upon, then pulled her over onto the bed.

"There, see? Wasn't that easy?" asked Timony.

"Yes," Bree admitted. "It only hurt a little, but the morphine kept me mostly comfortable."

"Good. It's doing its job, then."

A female doctor came in just as Ginger was leaving.

"Hi, my name is Doctor Kukraja." She didn't extend her hand but went directly to the computer. "I'm glad to see you in bed. I'm keeping you here overnight and then will re-evaluate you tomorrow. I want to make sure your medication is working and you're ready to go home."

Adam stood on the side of the bed with the window. "I'll have everything ready. Will she be able to walk up the stairs?"

"Probably, but not without pain. If you can arrange a room on the main floor that would be best," said the doctor.

"I'll see to it."

Bree frowned. "Where are you putting me? On a couch in the living room?"

Adam grinned. "No, I'm getting you a hospital bed and putting it in the family room off the kitchen. You'll be able to see Lilly that way and she can see you, too."

Adam had been nothing but kind. "That's nice of you. Thank you."

"I like to think I can take care of my wife. At least I'm trying to take care of you."

Doctor Kukraja folded her arms across her chest and observed her with Adam. Then she pointed at the recliner. "It's not very comfortable for sleeping, but it's slightly better than the floor.

Adam looked over at the recliner and shrugged. "It'll be fine."

Bree followed suit and gazed at the chair before she turned to Adam. "You don't have to stay. I'll probably be doing a lot of sleeping."

"Then I'll bring my Kindle and read. It'll be fine. I'm

not leaving you. I've already talked to Carole, and she's fine staying with Lilly until we return home."

That was news to Bree. "She is? What about her family?"

"It's just her and Gary now, and she said he can fend for himself for a few days."

Bree settled back onto her pillow. "Well, as long as it's Carole, I'm good with that. I won't worry as much. But I'm still going to worry until I get home and see her for myself."

"I figured you would. Now, why don't you just relax and let your pain medication do its work?"

Bree nodded. Her eyelids were heavy anyway, and though she was trying, she had a hard time keeping them open. She had more things she wanted to say, doggonit. "I love you, Adam." Her lids closed.

* * *

ADAM SMILED DOWN at his wife. He doubted she would even remember what she'd said, but he would never forget it. He had come to the realization some time ago that he loved her, too. He didn't know how to tell her, though. She would never believe him after what happened their disastrous first night together. Right now, that didn't matter. He would take care of her the best he could. He would keep Lilly near her but far enough away that she didn't inadvertently hurt her mother.

Yes, he loved his little wife. Theirs was a complicated relationship, but one he was willing to work at. He would have to work to get Bree to believe him. He would find a way to convince her his love was true. He just didn't know how.

* * *

BREE WAS HOME, but she had yet to see Lilly. She could barely walk, but refused to let Adam carry her. She knew that would be even more painful. The prescribed pain meds were potent, and she always slept after taking them. She was determined to take them only enough to stop the pain for a while. To be with Lilly, she would put up with the pain, however bad it got.

Adam walked beside her into the kitchen and then to the family room. He'd set up a hospital bed in there, and she couldn't wait to be in it. Her ribs were killing her. Every breath she took, no matter how shallow, hurt like crazy and every step was jarring.

She needed to be in bed and lay there without moving very much.

Bree had just climbed into the bed with Adam's help, when Carole came in with Lilly.

The baby looked at her and hollered, "Mama. Mama." She leaned her little body away from Carole and toward Bree.

Adam took Lilly from Carole. "I'll take her for now. Thank you so much, Carole. We owe you more than we can ever repay, for taking care of our heart."

"Yes, thank you so much," echoed Bree. She looked

at the remote and then adjusted the bed, so she was sitting up as much as possible. "Bring her closer, Adam. I want to kiss her and smell her baby smell."

"That's probably the Spaghetti-O's she had for lunch. I didn't have a chance to bathe her yet." Carole stood at the edge of the family room while Adam took Lilly from her.

Adam spoke to the baby. "Lilly, sweetie, Mama is hurt and not feeling good. You can kiss her, but she can't hold you right now. Do you understand? Mama is hurt."

"Mama. Mama. Mama." Lilly leaned her little body with her arms stretched toward Bree. "Mama. Mama."

"I told you she wouldn't understand." Tears filled Bree's eyes.

Adam leaned over and put Lilly close to Bree.

She kissed Lilly on the lips and then on her cheeks. Then she cupped her face. "Mama loves you, more than anything, baby girl." She leaned back so Lilly couldn't grab her. "Take her out, Adam," Bree turned away as the tears began to roll down her cheeks. "I need to sleep. I want to get better fast, because I don't know how long I'll be able to stop from cuddling her."

"It will be soon. You'll heal quickly."

He said it like he believed it.

Bree wanted desperately to believe it, too. She wasn't sure how long she'd be able to resist holding her child.

* * *

Two months later

Bree was meeting Stacy for tea. Finally healed enough that she could lift Lilly, she'd decided to take Stacy up on her offer for afternoon tea.

Bree packed a diaper bag and hauled it and Lilly out to the Navigator.

When they arrived at the Danvers residence, she was immediately shown into the living room.

Stacy was standing near a tea cart when Bree entered. She looked up. "Ah, there you are. Right on time. How are you feeling? Wade and I heard what happened to you. I'm so sorry you had something like that happen to you. I never did like Simon Chandler, but I never thought him capable of what happened to you. Please sit. And let me see that sweet girl." She held her arms out to Lilly.

Never shy, the baby went to Stacy right away.

Stacy laughed. "Oh, you are such a sweet girl. Yes, you are. That's right. You're a sweet girl." She looked over at Bree. "Is she always so friendly?"

Bree nodded. "She hasn't met anyone she didn't like yet. She always makes friends. I hope she keeps that up as she gets older."

They talked for a while.

Stacy gave Lilly a Vanilla Wafer cookie. "My children loved these when they were babies."

Lilly managed to mangle the cookie getting it soggy. Then it was just a matter of her trying to eat it and smearing most of it in her hands and on her face.

The baby tickled Stacy.

The older woman laughed delightedly.

"Are you sure you don't mind her getting so messy? She's likely to get the cookie all over your beautiful carpet."

Stacy waved an arm in front of her. "Don't worry about it. The carpet can be cleaned. And I haven't enjoyed myself this much in a long while."

When Lilly was done with the cookie, Stacy's butler appeared with a damp washcloth and Bree cleaned Lilly's face and hands.

Bree decided it was time to go. "I'd like her to get a nap before Adam gets home. He likes to play with her when he gets home."

"That's so good that he is a hands-on father. Wade was the same way. A lot of fathers simply let the wife raise the children, but we decided before we ever had children that we would both raise them. I believe that it's much better for the children when both parents are involved."

"Oh, we couldn't agree more. Adam and I both want to raise our children together. Thank you for a wonderful afternoon. Forgive me for not getting over here sooner, but I wanted to wait until I could bring Lilly with me."

Stacy raised her eyebrows just a little. "You couldn't help what happened to you. I hope they throw the book at Simon Chandler and his cohorts. I never did like that man."

"I didn't either. I felt sorry for Janie, but now she'll be able to divorce him without any repercussions."

"I saw her the other day." Stacy leaned forward. "She's already filed the paperwork to divorce him. Simon will still get what he came into the marriage with but little else because of the role he played in having you kidnapped. She said she thinks he could get more than twenty years for it. Plus when they married, her parents set it up so she would be well taken care of in the event of a divorce. They apparently weren't happy with the man she chose to marry."

"I can't say as I blame them for that. I think Simon has always been a tool."

"Most definitely."

Bree stood and picked up Lilly. "Thank you so much for having us over today. We had a great time. I'll have to remember about the Vanilla Wafers. Those, though messy, would be a good treat for Lilly once in a while."

Stacy stood and walked Bree to the door.

Bree's eyes widened. "I thought you had to use a wheelchair."

The older woman chuckled. "Only when I have to be on my feet a lot or walk a lot. Around the house I usually do fine. It's only when I go out that I need the wheelchair."

"Well, that's good. I'm glad you don't have to be in it all the time."

"So am I, my dear, so am I."

"Well, goodbye. We'll have to do this again soon."

"I agree. I'll give you a call in a couple of weeks."

"That sounds great. Bye! Bye!" Bree gazed down at

Lilly. "Can you wave bye to Miss Stacy, sweetheart? Bye. Say bye."

"Bah," said Lilly.

"She did it!" Bree was thrilled. That was her third word, behind mama and no. She'd gotten that one down really well and she knew what each of the words meant. Lilly wasn't just parroting what was said. She understood.

Bree couldn't wait to get home to tell Adam.

* * *

"COME TO MAMA, baby girl. Come on, you can do it." Bree watched Lilly get up after falling and walk over. "That's my girl." She lifted Lilly high into the air and then turned in a circle while holding her.

Bree was still so happy she was allowed to pick up Lilly and hold her after weeks of not doing so, that she did it all the time.

Adam laughed from the doorway to the nursery. "I figured I'd find you here." His smile faded and his mouth formed a flat line. "Bree, I'd like to talk to you. Can you put Lilly in her playpen for a moment, please?"

"Um, yeah, sure." She carried Lilly to the playpen and set her in the middle of it. This one was sturdier than the one in the family room, which Lilly had managed to topple over twice now. Luckily for Bree, Lilly didn't mind being in the playpen. She played with all her favorite toys at once, which she delighted in.

"Where would you like to talk?"

"The bedroom…my bedroom, if you please."

Bree stiffened and nodded, heading out to his bedroom. *What could he want to say in his bedroom that can't be said in the nursery? It's not like Lilly will understand what he's saying.*

There, he had several bouquets of roses spread throughout the room, with a single rose on the bed.

She looked around the room. "I don't understand, Adam. What is all of this?" When she turned back to Adam, she saw he was on one knee.

"Bree Kincaid, would you do me the great honor of marrying me and becoming my wife, for real this time? I love you, Bree. I will never love anyone else. I won't cheat or lie, and I'll do my best not to die too early. Say you'll marry me, Bree."

CHAPTER 12

Bree stared down at Adam on his knee. He held another ring, this one a double anniversary band with all three of their birthstones interspersed with the two bands of diamonds.

"Bree?"

He looked so earnest, kneeling there with his heart in his eyes.

Her eyes teared and she reached over and cupped his beloved face. "Yes, Adam, I'll—"

Adam whooped, bounded up, and wrapped her in his arms.

His lips found hers, and this kiss was more than she could have hoped for. Every bit of longing was in his kiss. Every bit of love and commitment and celebration was in his kiss.

He broke the kiss. "I love you, Bree. I think I've loved you forever but was afraid to tell you. I'm not afraid anymore. I want to shout it to the world, write it across the sky, and take out a full-page ad in every newspaper, proclaiming my love for you." He wrapped her tighter in his arms and lifted her, swinging her in a circle.

She laughed and held on for the ride. He slowed and put her down. She reached up and cupped his face between her palms. "Adam, I love you more than I thought possible. You've made all my dreams come true, giving me Lilly and now you. I couldn't ask for more."

"When do you want to renew our vows? Do you want a big wedding? Do you—"

"I don't need another ceremony. What I need is a wedding night. I don't ever want to be out of your arms again. I want to sleep beside you every night and wake up with you every morning. That's all I want." She pressed her lips against his. This was her first kiss she initiated as a wife in love with her husband. The first of many.

Bree looked around the room at all the flowers and smiled. Adam had taken her love of flowers and set the mood to something she would love. She couldn't imagine a more romantic and loving proposal.

Lilly hollered and cried.

Bree listened for a moment. Then she kissed Adam, her kiss full of her love for him. "Time to get our little girl. She's growing by leaps and bounds. She won't be a baby much longer. She's almost a year old now. Where did the time go?"

"But, my darling bride, she's not the last baby we'll

have. I want to start working on that as soon as possible." He winked at her.

She was both scandalized and flattered at the same time. Bree shook her head and then laughed. "I'd like nothing more than to work on having a baby with you and giving Lilly a little brother or sister. "

"Good." He placed a soft kiss on her mouth. "Let's get Lilly and play with her until her nap time. Then we can take a nap, too." He waggled his eyebrows.

"I think a nap sounds like a wonderful idea." She wrapped her arms around his neck and placed her lips on his, kissing him with all the love in her heart. She couldn't wait for nap time to show him how she felt. When she pulled back, she saw Adam was smiling. That was the thing she wanted to see most...him smiling at her.

She took his hand, and they walked back to Lilly's room to spend some quality time with their precious daughter.

* * *

ONE MONTH later

LILLY SAT IN HER HIGHCHAIR, a chocolate cupcake with one candle on it was in front of her.

"Come on, baby girl. You can blow it out. Mommy and Daddy will help."

Bree and Adam, one standing on either side of Lilly, jointly blew out the candle on the sweet treat.

Then Bree took the candle from the treat and handed the cupcake to Lilly who took it and smashed it in her hand before getting some into in her mouth.

Adam laughed.

So did Bree. "She'll need a bath after this."

"We can do it together. I love watching her play in the tub. She enjoys it so much. I only hope our first child together is as good-natured as Lilly. I have a feeling the next child will be a Beelzebub in comparison."

Bree placed two fingers on his lips. "Shh, you'll curse us."

He kissed her fingers.

Since he'd asked her to marry him again, they'd spent every night together making love and cuddling, even in their sleep.

Bree couldn't remember sleeping better. She woke every morning with a smile.

Adam told her he felt the same way. He'd actually dreaded going into the office, so he'd left Emily in charge. He worked from home and what he couldn't do there, he did on his weekly visit downtown.

Sometimes Bree and Lilly drove behind him to the office and shopped until noon. Then he would take them somewhere fun for lunch. Afterward, Bree headed home a put Lilly down for her nap while she took one herself.

She tired easily lately and needed the nap in the afternoon to be chipper when Adam returned.

On the days he was home, they'd taken to napping when Lilly did on a regular basis.

Not until Bree missed her monthly—or Riding the Crimson Stallion, as she referred to it—did she take a pregnancy test. Seeing the result, she had to be sure and took a second test. Both had the same result. Positive. She was pregnant.

She started to whoop and holler and then remembered that Lilly was sleeping. Tossing the tests into the trash, she hurried downstairs to ask Carole to prepare Adam's favorite meal. He grew up on a ranch and was a meat-and-potatoes kind of guy. His mother's meatloaf was his favorite thing in the world. Madelyn gave Carole the recipe so she could make it for Adam.

They hadn't had it for a long time, so meatloaf and mashed potatoes were on the menu, along with a German chocolate cake for dessert.

She couldn't wait for him to arrive home.

* * *

BREE WAS ABSOLUTELY giddy by the time Adam arrived home.

When he came through the door from the garage into the kitchen, he stopped and sniffed. "Is that meatloaf I smell?" He sniffed again. "If it's not it is the second most wonderful thing I've ever smelled."

She laughed and walked over to him from her spot

by Lilly in the family room. She wrapped her arms around his waist. "Hi, there."

"Hi, there." He leaned down and kissed her forehead. "Did you have a good day?"

"From the looks of you. I definitely had a better day than you did."

"I'm just tired. The day wasn't bad, just busy. That happens when you only go into the office one day a week."

"Do you want to go in more than one day?" Bree didn't want him to, but she also knew that he needed to do what was necessary for his business.

Adam frowned. "Why would I want to do that? I love being home with you and Lilly." He placed his arms around her. "So tell me about your day instead."

"Well," Bree hesitated. "You remember how we started working on expanding our family as soon as you proposed?"

"I remember. As a matter of fact, I remember just about every time we've worked on expanding the family. Why do you ask?"

"Because I believe the night you proposed we got a second blessing." She took his hand and placed it on her lower belly. "We're going to have a baby."

Adam was slow to grin, but when he did, it was devastating. "A baby."

"Yup. Lilly is going to have a little brother or sister. What do you think?" She was pretty sure he was as thrilled as she was, he was smiling after all.

Suddenly he picked her up and swung her in a

circle. "We're having another baby!" He grinned and then slowly let her slide down him to the floor. "That's the best news ever. How do you think Lilly will feel about it?"

"I think she'll be thrilled. It will be like having a live baby doll. She'll want to dress him up—"

His eyes widened. "Him? Do you know what it is already?"

She chuckled. "No, silly. I just don't want to be calling him an it, so I'm saying him."

He chuckled. "Right. Of course."

She gazed up at him, a hint of worry in her mind. "Our family is expanding. Are you happy?"

He hugged her closer. "Yes. I want us to have more children, I just wasn't expecting it so soon. I mean in the back of my mind, I knew it was a possibility, but how often does it happen so quickly? We made love several times that first night, but still…"

"Probably more often than we can imagine. Anyway, in celebration I asked Carole to prepare your favorite meal…your mom's meatloaf. We haven't had it since I moved in, so I'm looking forward to it, too. Come on. Let's get our daughter. She needs to be fed and put to bed. Then we can have a quiet dinner, just the two of us."

"Sounds good. I might even have time to romance my wife before dinner."

They walked into the family room, picked up Lilly and put their plan into effect.

Bree was as anxious as Adam for a little romancing before dinner and after, too.

* * *

THREE WEEKS later

ADAM LOOKED weary when Bree saw him.

She went to him and hugged him. "Are you okay? You don't look okay."

He told her what had happened, leaving nothing out.

"I'm sorry your day sucked, but I have a surprise. Come on." She took his hand and pulled him into the family room.

Lilly sat on a blanket in the middle of the floor.

They'd pushed the furniture back close to the walls and fashioned a gate in front of the fireplace.

The middle of the room was bare except for the blanket and Lilly's toys.

"Lilly, look who's home."

The baby looked over at her parents. "Dada. Dada. Dada."

Adam grinned as wide as his face.

Bree had been working extra hard to get her to say *dada,* but the stubborn little thing she was, she refused and called him mama instead.

He lifted Lilly in the air above his head and jiggled her a little bit.

She screamed with laughter.

Then he brought her down and held her with his arm under her butt. "You made Daddy very happy. Who's Daddy's girl?" He tickled her. "Who's Daddy's girl?"

"Lilee," she said.

Adam's eyes widened and he looked at Bree. "She said her name. She knows who she is."

Nodding, Bree's eyes filled with tears.

Lilly had been chattering for months with mama being the only word that Bree and Adam understood. Now she was talking. Saying new words every day.

How would she react to a new baby? Would she be jealous? Excited?

She wouldn't understand where the baby came from but she would understand when the baby was here.

Was Bree ready for another baby?

Should they have waited until Lilly was out of diapers?

Adam put his free arm around Bree's waist and snugged her close. "What are you thinking about? I can see your mind whirling a mile a minute."

She looked up at her husband, then at her daughter in his arm, and realized nothing else mattered. These two were her heart and she loved them more than life itself. The new baby would only add to her happiness.

"I was thinking about our family," she answered honestly. "You two are my heart. I love you more than I can ever express."

Adam's gaze softened. "I feel the same way, my love."

She realized then that her dreams had come true. Not as she expected them, that was true. But it was perfect all the same.

Bree smiled at her husband. "I love you."

"I love you, too. What brought that on?"

"I was just thinking how wonderful my life turned out to be and how happy I am."

He grinned. "That was awfully schmaltzy."

"I can live with that."

$$* * *$$

THE FOLLOWING day Adam received a call and headed to his office to take it, leaving Bree with a sleepy Lilly in the family room.

When Lilly finally conked out and Adam wasn't back yet, Bree sought him out in his office.

"Yes, I understand. Thank you for calling." He set his phone on the desk and looked up at Bree. "That was the DA. Simon has pleaded guilty to stealing secrets from Danvers. I didn't even know he'd been doing that." He ran a hand through his hair, making it stand on end in spots. "Anyway, the kidnapping charge is off the table. He'll still spend time in prison, just not as much. And we don't have to testify."

Bree sat in one of the leather chairs across from his desk. "Well, not testifying is a good thing. I wasn't looking forward to it. We can go about our lives and not think about Simon anymore."

"That's true. I want to discuss something else with you. What have you been thinking about your garden center? Do you still want to do it? Is it something you'd like to table for now. I want you to do whatever makes you happy."

"Well, my writing has been taking off and I've sort of put the garden center on the back burner. I want to concentrate on my writing. It's proving to be very lucrative, and I want to keep at it. So, if I do the garden center, and that looks less and less likely, it will be years down the road.

EPILOGUE

en Years Later

"Lilly! You get out of that tree." She couldn't believe that her daughter had grown so much. Lilly was already almost as tall as she was, and she was only eleven. By the time she stopped growing, she'd be several inches taller than Bree.

"But, Mom."

"Don't 'but Mom' me. Get down and come here."

Bree was setting the patio table for dinner. "You know your grandparents will be here any minute. I don't want them to see you climbing a tree in a dress."

Lilly climbed down and walked over to her mother; her shoulders slumped. "I don't see why it matters. Grandma lets me climb the trees at her house."

Bree placed her hands on her hips. "Grandma and I

are having a talk about that, too. Either way it doesn't matter. You know your brother and sister will try to follow you, and they are too little. What if one of them fell? Did you ever think about that?"

"No." She hung her head and kicked at an invisible rock. "How would you feel if they did?"

"Bad. I don't want them to be hurt."

Lilly's mouth quivered, and tears glistened in her eyes.

"Honey, I don't think you realize how much they idolize you. They want to do anything you can do, only they aren't big enough yet." Bree thought back to their first baby. Their son, Theodore. They were going to call him Teddy, but he was stillborn.

Bree's heart still hurt when she thought of him. They didn't try again for years because Bree was afraid, and she didn't think she could survive if it happened again. When she was alone, she still cried. The picture of Teddy in his tiny coffin was more than enough to send her into a crying jag for days.

Finally, about five years ago, they decided to try for another baby, and they were blessed this time with Sarah. She was blonde and blue-eyed like Bree and almost as sweet as Lilly had been.

Lilly was excited at the idea of a baby sister and doted on Sarah.

For her part, Sarah now loved Lilly best and wanted to do all the things she did, good or bad, like climbing the trees. Even though she knew her little legs couldn't reach the branches yet.

Jamie came along three years ago, and he was a boy's boy and his father's mini-me. He had Adam's dark hair and blue eyes. He was rough and tumble, always getting into things, including trouble, and was the first to follow Lilly in an adventure. Whether it was playing cowboys in the back yard, which they'd had fenced, or getting into the cookie jar after Carole made fresh cookies, he was there.

And now, Bree was expecting again. Even with Sarah and Jamie's births being perfectly—almost text-book—normal, she still worried. She wondered if she could have done something or if there was some sign that she missed.

Every pregnancy since Teddy's was accompanied by a healthy dose of fear. Would it happen again?

Bree did her best to shove her fears aside. She had three wonderful, healthy children, an understanding husband, and a wonderful life. Still...

The children were playing on the lawn, and Adam was at the grill when the first hard labor pain hit. She closed her eyes and waited for it to pass. It lasted less than a minute.

Adam was beside her in a second. "What is it? Are you in labor?"

Bree nodded. "I just started, so it won't be for a while though. The kids can play for a bit longer, but you should call your parents and have them come. They'll have to wait for a while, but I don't think they'll mind."

He sat next to her. "They never mind coming to see

the kids. They could probably do without seeing us, but that's neither here nor there." He reached into his pocket for his phone and placed the call to his parents. "They'll be here in an hour. Is that soon enough?"

Bree nodded. "That should be fine. Now, sit back and watch the kids play tag. I just had to make Lilly get out of a tree, so she decided to do something the little ones can enjoy with her."

"She's a good sister."

"That she is."

They watched the kids, with Bree's pain coming about every twelve to fifteen minutes.

Less than an hour later, Madelyn and Rocky joined them in the backyard. Both gave Bree a kiss on the forehead and a hug, then poured themselves iced tea from the pitcher on the table.

"How are you, Bree?" Madelyn sipped her drink.

"I'm good. You know how I am, you've been through this six times," she said with a laugh.

"Yes, but everyone is different. For me, the pregnancy was somewhat difficult, especially with Megan, but the delivery was a breeze. With you, it is the exact opposite, so in that case, I guess I do understand."

"I was thinking about Teddy." Saying it out loud made her eyes tear up.

Madelyn placed a hand on Bree's arm. "Sweetheart, nothing is happening to this baby. It's going to be just fine."

"Have you found out the sex yet?" asked Rocky. "We could use another boy, just to even things out." He shrugged his shoulders when Madelyn furrowed her brows at him. "What?" He stared at his wife. "I'm just saying…"

Bree smiled. "Well, I'll do the best I can but that's sort of out of my hands." She looked over at Adam.

He simply grinned.

They all laughed.

Suddenly, Bree closed her eyes as the pain hit, taking over her concentration and conversation skills.

Adam frowned. "It's been less than six minutes since the last contraction. I think we should prepare to head to the hospital."

Bree nodded. "I think we should get ready to go. Something isn't right."

He took her hand and kissed it. "Sweetheart, everything will be fine. He's just a little anxious to get here, that's all."

She nodded. "I know you're right, but I—"

Adam kneeled in front of her. "Darling don't fixate on what might go wrong. Teddy's birth was an unusual happening. You know that."

"My brain does know that, but my heart can't see that far, even though it's been so long."

Adam helped her to her feet. "Everything will be fine. We'll have a beautiful baby, and our family will be complete. You'll see."

"I know. I'll be better."

He looked at his parents. "Will you stay out here with the kids while we get ready to go?"

"Do you really have to ask?" asked his mother. "You know we will. Just tell us when you're leaving."

Adam nodded. "We will. Come on, sweetheart. Let's get you inside."

Bree looked over at her in-laws. "Thank you both. We truly appreciate you being here for them." Her gaze swung to where her children had pitched themselves onto the lush green lawn. "It looks like they are having fun. We'll come say goodbye to everyone before we go."

Putting his hand at the small of her back, Adam looked at her up and down. "Maybe you should lie down for a bit. You look a little pale."

She shook her head. "I'm fine, just a bit tired but I can't get comfortable lying down. If I manage to, a pain will hit, and I'll have to go through it all again. I'd rather not do that."

"Okay, sit on the recliner. I'll get your bag for the hospital and then be right back down."

She waved him off just as another pain hit. She looked at her watch—four minutes. At this rate, they wouldn't make it to the hospital before the baby was born.

By the time he returned, she was back to normal, but a little anxious.

"Are you ready? Do you need anything else besides your hospital bag?"

She shook her head. "Everything is in there, including stuff for the new baby." She tried to get up from the recliner but failed.

Adam took her hands and pulled her up.

"Thank you. It will be nice to be able to rise from a chair when I need to, without your help."

"Oh, but my darling bride, I always want to help you."

"You just say that to be charming."

He waggled his brows. "You know I'm the king of charming."

She barked out a laugh. "I guess you are, at that. Let's say goodbye to everyone and then I want to get to the hospital fast, but you don't need to break any land speed records."

Adam placed a hand over his heart. "Who me? I never speed, you know that."

"Ha," she blurted. "You speed anytime you think you can get away with it."

He chuckled. "You're right, but I will be a good boy today."

"Okay, let's go." Another pain hit, and she stopped and made her breathing even. "I think we'll have to call and say goodbye because you might have to hurry after all. This one seems anxious to get here."

"Gotcha." Adam put the overnight bag's strap on his shoulder and assisted Bree to the car. He took her to the Mercedes SUV and lifted her into the passenger seat.

Because of her belly, she couldn't buckle the seat belt.

He hurried around to the driver's side and got behind the wheel. After buckling up, he backed out of the garage and headed to the hospital as fast as he could.

Bree called her mother-in-law. "We had to leave right away, but I did want to tell the kids bye." She listened to Madelyn on the phone. "Yes, Adam will call after the baby's here."

She nodded even though Madelyn couldn't see that. "Tell Rocky I haven't forgotten his request for a boy. We love you all, but I have to go now."

Bree ended the call in the middle of a contraction. "Adam, hurry, please."

He looked over at her. "You got it." He pressed the gas pedal, and the car sped up.

Adam parked at the ER door and helped Bree inside before taking the car to the parking lot.

By the time he returned, he saw Bree sat in a wheelchair, headed through the doors into the ER rooms.

"Wait. I'm coming with you," he called as he ran after them.

An hour later, Bree was in the birthing room, pushing to deliver the new baby.

After about thirty minutes, Matthew "Matty" Kincaid arrived and was placed on his mother's stomach.

"Adam." Bree looked at him for a moment. "He has my blonde hair."

"He does."

A nurse came over. "We need to take him, clean him up and swaddle him so he doesn't get cold. He'll be back before you miss him." The nurse picked up Matty and placed him in the crook of her arm. "We'll be right back."

Bree couldn't stop the tears that rolled down her cheeks.

Adam said nothing, but he leaned over, took her in his arms, and held her while she cried.

"Excuse me," said the same nurse. "I have a little someone for you."

Matty wore a little blue-and-white striped hat on his head.

He looked so cute; Bree kissed his cheeks before settling him in her arms. "Hello, Matty. How are you, my darling son?"

Adam chuckled. "You asked each of our children that very question when they were born, and not a one of them answered you."

"You never know, one of them might someday."

Adam's eyebrows shot high up his forehead. "You want more children? I thought we'd stop after this one."

She laughed. "You should see your face." She decided to put him out of his misery. "I'm not planning to have any more children. I'm almost forty, and I don't want to be retired and still have children in high school."

He swiped the back of his hand over his forehead. "Whew. You had me worried there."

She noticed Adam's shock had settled into a smile as he stared at his new son. "I'd like some time for just us. We need that. Now, it's all about the children, as it should be, but later, I want it to be just us."

He turned his gaze toward her, his eyes twinkling, and his smile still in place. "You are an amazing woman, my love. You know just what to say to ease my mind."

She reached out and entwined her fingers with his. "I love you, Adam, more today than yesterday but not as much as tomorrow."

"I love you, too, Bree. More than I ever thought possible."

She looked down at Matty.

The baby stared. At least, it looked like he stared at Bree. He had big blue eyes and blonde hair so pale it looked white. He was the most beautiful child Bree had ever seen...at least, since the birth of her other children.

Bree was happier than she'd ever thought possible. She wouldn't trade her life for anything. Not any of it, because she had to go through the bad times to have the good times and be where she was now. A wife and mother. Her dreams really did come true.

COMING SOON!

THE RANCHER
Colorado Billionaires
Book 2

Ray Kincaid stood with one foot on the bottom rail and his left arm resting on the top rail of the three railed white wooden fence surrounding the racing track. In his right hand, he held a stopwatch. He watched his fourteen-year-old daughter, Maddy, as she raced her horse, White Lightning, around the track.

He was proud of how far she'd come and yet terrified she'd die like her mother had. Francie had been a great rider...an excellent jockey, but that didn't stop her from dying when her horse lost its footing and stumbled, throwing her over its head, breaking her neck.

Maddy had only been three at the time. She was the only thing that held Ray together. He had to raise her.

He couldn't wallow in grief because he had Maddy to take care of. She'd saved him. One little three-year-old girl, who he loved more than life, had saved him from falling into ruin.

Behind him, he heard the gravel crunching under the tires of a vehicle. He turned and watched, prepared to tell whoever he didn't work on Sundays.

The car was a dark blue, older model, Chevy Yukon. The driver's side door opened, and a statuesque redhead stepped out. She closed the door and headed toward him. Wearing faded jeans that looked like they were painted on, a plain emerald-green t-shirt and cowboy boots, she looked like she belonged on a ranch.

She walked up to him. "Excuse me. Are you Ray Kincaid?"

"I am, but I don't take visitors on Sundays."

"I'm not a visitor. I'm Lyris Jennings your new vet." She held out her right hand. "Pleased to meet you."

Ray took her outstretched hand. "I wasn't expecting you until tomorrow."

She shrugged and pulled her hand back. "I made better time than I anticipated and rather than spend the night in a hotel in Denver, I decided to come on out. If you'd rather I come back tomorrow, I can do that."

Ray thought about it for a moment. He was tempted to tell her just that, but it was ridiculous for her to spend the money on a hotel room when the guesthouse was ready to be occupied. "No, don't do that. Your quarters are ready. I've put you in the guesthouse. As soon as Maddy is done caring for her horse, we'll take you to it and let you get settled in. Supper is at seven in the main house. We all eat together. Breakfast is at six and lunch is at noon. There is always food in the fridge and the cupboards if you get hungry between meals. Maddy and I usually have hot cocoa before bed. You're welcome to come to the library and join us."

"Thank you, I might take you up on that." She turned her attention to the racetrack. "She rides very well. And that's a beautiful horse. I love the lightning bolt blazing down his nose against the black of his coat. It's mesmerizing."

"His name is White Lightning because of that blaze, although with how Maddy has been training him, he runs like lightning."

"She looked good enough to ride professionally. Is that her plan?" Dr. Jennings leaned against the fence with her foot on the lowest rail.

The smile Ray had been feeling from the pride in Maddy's riding slipped away, replaced by fear. What if the same thing happened to her as happened to Francie? He couldn't get the thought out of his mind. He knew he was being unfair to Maddy, but he wanted her safe. She was his baby girl. Always was and always would be.

"I didn't realize you actually saw her ride. You didn't get here in time for that."

"I watched from the road before I drove up. As I said, she's very good."

Ray nodded. "She is. She's just as good as her mother was."

The woman cocked her head to one side. "Was? I didn't realize—"

"As long as you're going to be working and living here, you should know. Francie, my wife, died in a riding accident. She was thrown from a horse and broke her neck. Maddy was three at the time."

The doctor looked at him with concern, but there was no pity in her eyes. "I'm so sorry. That must have been hard for you. Raising a child alone isn't easy."

Ray shifted from foot to foot. He didn't know why he was nervous. "No, it's not."

The sides of her mouth turned up. "You must be proud of her."

He nodded. "I am. Very proud. She's only fourteen and she rides as well as someone who's been doing it much longer. I just..."

She frowned for just a moment. "You just wish she'd chosen something else. I'm sure her riding, especially racing, would make you very nervous considering how your wife passed away."

"It does, but I can't quash her dream. This is what she wants and she's good at it. If she continues, she'll be great by the time she's sixteen and old enough to race professionally. She's already got the build for it. She's only four feet eleven inches and ninety-eight pounds. Of course, she might hit a growth spurt, but I doubt it. She's too much like her mother." He smiled at a memory that came to him unbidden. "She was a little thing just like Maddy. I was terrified when she told me she was expecting. I'm so big and she was just a tiny, little woman. She assured me it would be okay. And she was right. She didn't have any problem giving birth." He turned his gaze and his body toward the new veterinarian. "I have no idea why I just shared that."

Lyris reached over and laid a hand on his arm. "It's all right. People often share things with me they wouldn't otherwise. It must be something about my face." She smiled.

Ray looked at her and felt the world tilt a little. She was so different from Francie. From her bright red hair to her lush curves and her long legs. Lyris was a good five eleven, only five inches shorter than he was, instead of nearly a foot-and-a-half like Francie had been.

But he'd loved her with his whole heart and now Maddy filled his heart with joy…and fear. He wouldn't deny it, but he would do whatever he could to ease it by teaching her to tumble. He'd enrolled her in gymnastics as a toddler and had her keep after it.

Maddy liked it well enough, but it wasn't her love. That was racing. She wanted to be a jockey almost more than she wanted her next breath.

As for Lyris, was her face why he told her what he did? He wasn't so stupid as to not realize she was a beautiful woman. She had big emerald eyes, a bow-shaped mouth, a heart-shaped face, and all that red hair.

Yes, he was definitely attracted to her, but she was

his employee or would be if they came to an understanding about her duties. They didn't amount to much…keep his horses healthy. That was her only job.

They approached the barn.

Maddy came running out to him. "Did you see? Daddy, did you see? White Lightning beat his best record. He's ready to race."

"I thought you wanted to wait until you were old enough to ride him?"

She vigorously shook her head. "That won't be for more than six months. I can't make him wait that long. Johnny can ride him. He has before and I know he's the best."

Lyris perked up. "Johnny? Do you have Johnny Cantoni riding for you? How did you manage that?"

Maddy looked at her with furrowed brows. "Who are you?"

Ray did the introductions. "Maddy, this is Lyris Jennings, the new vet." He turned toward Lyris. "This is my daughter Maddy. She's fifteen going on thirty."

Maddy gave her father the stink eye, then turned back toward Lyris. "I thought you were going to be a man. What kind of name is Lyris?"

The woman chuckled and extended her right hand. "I'm pleased to meet you, Maddy. My name originates from the Greek name for a lyra."

Maddy ignored her hand. "I know what a lyra is. It's a small, harp-like instrument and was used in ancient Greece. We just learned about that in our world history class."

"I didn't think they taught that in schools anymore." Lyris put her hands in her jeans pockets.

Maddy shrugged. "It's an elective. They want to get us used to college, so our classes are listed in mods of twenty minutes. The class is usually two-to-three mods. And we get to have electives, like choir, art, or world history, stuff like that."

Lyris pursed her lips and nodded. "I think that's a great idea. Less culture shock when you go to college."

"That's the plan. We've been doing it for about ten years, so I guess it's working," said Maddy. "I'm hungry. I'm going to wash up and then see what Henrietta has cooking." She took off and raced toward the house.

"She's quite the handful," said Lyris.

"That she is." Ray smiled. "But I wouldn't have her any other way. So, tell me what your plans for my animals are?"

"I want to keep them healthy and safe. There has been talk in the veterinarian circles about someone doping the animals. Have you heard anything?"

"No. And if it was one of my people I would know. Most all of them have been here for years and love the horses as much as I do."

As they approached the door to the kitchen, Lyris took her hands from her pockets but kept them at her sides. "Well, we should both keep our eyes open. Especially at the racetrack. Some people will do anything to win and if the rest of your horses run anything like White Lightning, they'll be prime targets."

Ray let out a sigh and then ran a hand behind his

neck. "If it's not one thing it's another. Sometimes I think the gods are against me." He held the door open for her and then followed her in, making sure the door closed behind him.

"I want to start the horses on a vitamin and mineral regime as soon as possible."

"Why? I've never had the need for that in all the years I've been in business and my horses are healthy."

"And I want to keep them that way. I want them to be as strong as possible, especially with these doping rumors going around. You'll find that you can't trust anyone. You might find out that one of your employees has a gambling problem and needs the money to pay off loan sharks or something. You don't know what is going on in everyone's lives."

Ray heard voices in the kitchen. Maddy was asking about breakfast from Gwen, his housekeeper and cook. He turned to Lyris. "I don't want Maddy to know about the doping. Say nothing about it to her if you want to keep your job."

She stiffened. "I would never, but I guess you don't really know that do you. I would never hurt her or any child on purpose. And that is all that knowledge would do. It would hurt her. She'd be afraid to give White Lightning his chance and then she'd regret it. I can't do that to her."

He narrowed his eyes. "How is it you think you know my daughter so well?"

"Because I see a lot of me in her. I was just like her

when I was her age, and I know things happened that changed my life, not necessarily for the better."

Ray gazed at his daughter. "She's already lost so much and even though she was so young, I know it changed her. I've done the best I could, and Gwen has helped just by being here and being a sounding board for both of us. Despite that, I often wonder if I shouldn't have remarried just to give her a mother."

"I don't know the answer to that, but marrying only for that reason wouldn't have been good for either of you, or for the woman you chose. You've done a remarkable job raising her. Don't second guess yourself."

Ray smiled. "You're a little bossy for being a new employee."

She looked at him with her eyes narrowed and her hands on her hips. "I'm a contractor. I'm not actually your employee and we should get that settled right now. We can discuss things and ultimately, I'll have to acquiesce to your demands, but that doesn't mean I won't fight you for what is best for the horses."

"I only want what's best for my animals. All of them, but that doesn't mean I won't stand up for my rights as their owner."

"I won't give in to you just because you're their owner. I will make my feelings on the subject known and fight for what I think is right."

Ray cocked a brow. "Well, I guess we'll see who wins won't we."

"I guess we will."

"Don't get too comfortable, Lyris, I figure we'll have definite fights coming up and I want you to be prepared for them." Ray laughed at her expression.

Her eyes were narrowed and her face was turning pink.

He liked it and liked her. She was the first woman who'd actually shown him some backbone, and he liked it a lot. But would she stay and fight with him or leave like most of the other women he dated?

THE RANCHER COMING IN MARCH 2025!

ABOUT THE AUTHOR

Cynthia Woolf is a USA Today Bestselling Author and an award-winning author of sixty-six historical western romance novels, two time-travel western romance novels, nine contemporary western romance novels, one contemporary western novellas, and six sci-fi romance novels, which she calls westerns in space.

Along with these books she has also published twelve boxed sets of her books. Montana Billionaires, The Tame Series, Destiny in Deadwood, The Marshals Mail Order Brides, The Brides of the Oregon Trail series, Centauri Series and Swords and Blasters.

Cynthia loves writing and reading romance. Her first western romance Tame A Wild Heart was inspired by the story her mother told her of meeting Cynthia's father on a ranch in Creede, Colorado. Although Tame A Wild Heart takes place in Creede that is the only similarity between the stories. Her father was a cowboy, not a bounty hunter, and her mother was a nursemaid (called a nanny now), not the owner of the ranch.

Cynthia credits her wonderfully supportive

husband Jim and her great critique partners for saving her sanity and allowing her to explore her creativity.

STAY CONNECTED!

Newsletter
Want to hear about coming books first?
Sign up for my <u>newsletter</u> and get a free book.

Follow Cynthia

https://facebook.com/CynthiaWoolf
https://twitter.com/CynthiaWoolf
http://cynthiawoolf.com

Don't forget if you love the book, I'd appreciate it if you could leave a review at the retailer you purchased the book from.
Thanks so much,
Cynthia

ALSO BY CYNTHIA WOOLF

Colorado Brides
THE CEO

The Brides of the Klondike
The Gold Rush Bride (Available in German)
The Gold Mountain Bride

* * *

Christmas at the Mistletoe Inn
Cooking Up Christmas

* * *

The Prescott Brides
A Bride for Ross (Available in German)
A Bride for Frank (Available in German)
A Bride for Tucker (Available in German)
A Bride for Clay (Available in German)
A Bride for Brodie (Available in German)

* * *

Billionaire Cowboys

Her Secret Cowboy Billionaire (Available in German)

Her Mysterious Cowboy Billionaire (Available in German)

Her Royal Cowboy Billionaire (Available in German)

Her Bachelor Cowboy Billionaire (Available in German)

Her Christmas Cowboy Billionaire (Available in German)

Her Wild Cowboy Billionaire (Available in German)

Her Elusive Cowboy Billionaire

Her Disguised Cowboy Billionaire

* * *

Heart Wish series

Heart of Stone

Heart of Shadow

Heart of Silver

* * *

Bachelors and Babies

Carter

* * *

Cupids & Cowboys

Lanie

* * *

Brides of Golden City

A Husband for Victoria

A Husband for Cordelia

A Husband for Adeline

* * *

The Brides of Homestead Canyon

A Family for Christmas

Kissed by a Stranger

Thorpe's Mail Order Bride

* * *

The Marshal's Mail Order Brides (Available in German)

The Carson City Bride

The Virginia City Bride

The Silver City Bride

The Eureka City Bride

* * *

Bride of Nevada

Genevieve

* * *

Brides of the Oregon Trail

Hannah **(Available in German)**

Lydia **(Available in German)**

Bella **(Available in German)**

Eliza **(Available in German)**

Rebecca **(Available in German)**

Charlotte **(Available in German)**

Amanda **(Available in German)**

Emma Rose **(Available in German)**

Nora **(Available in German)**

Opal

* * *

Brides of San Francisco (Available in German)

Nellie

Annie

Cora

Sophia

Amelia

Violet

* * *

Brides of Seattle (Available in German)

Mail Order Mystery

Mail Order Mayhem

Mail Order Mix-Up

Mail Order Moonlight

Mail Order Melody

* * *

Brides of Tombstone (Available in German)

Mail Order Outlaw

Mail Order Doctor

Mail Order Baron

* * *

Central City Brides (Available in German)

The Dancing Bride

The Sapphire Bride

The Irish Bride

The Pretender Bride

* * *

Destiny in Deadwood (Available in German)

Jake

Liam

Zach

* * *

Hope's Crossing (Available in German)

The Stolen Bride

The Hunter Bride

The Replacement Bride

The Unexpected Bride

* * *

Matchmaker & Co Series (Available in German)
Capital Bride

Heiress Bride

Fiery Bride

Colorado Bride

Troubled Bride

* * *

The Surprise Brides
Gideon

* * *

Tame (Available in German)
Tame a Wild Heart

Tame a Wild Wind

Tame a Wild Bride

Tame A Honeymoon Heart

Tame Boxset

* * *

Centauri Series (SciFi Romance)
Centauri Dawn

Centauri Twilight

Centauri Midnight

* * *

The Swords of Gregory (SciFi Romance)

Jenala

Riza

Honora

* * *

Singles

Sweetwater Springs Christmas

www.ingramcontent.com/pod-product-compliance
Lightning Source LLC
Chambersburg PA
CBHW040225170726
48295CB00014B/810